Young**Writers**

what's the story?

WALES VOL II

Edited by Chris Hallam

First published in Great Britain in 2004 by
YOUNG WRITERS
Remus House,
Coltsfoot Drive,
Peterborough, PE2 9JX
Telephone (01733) 890066

SB ISBN 1 84460 312 1

FOREWORD

This year, Young Writers proudly presents a showcase of the best short stories and creative writing from today's up-and-coming writers.

We set the challenge of writing for one of our four themes - 'General Short Stories', 'Ghost Stories', 'Tales With A Twist' and 'A Day In The Life Of . . .'. The effort and imagination expressed by each individual writer was more than impressive and made selecting entries an enjoyable, yet demanding, task.

What's The Story? Wales Vol II is a collection that we feel you are sure to enjoy - featuring the very best young authors of the future. Their hard work and enthusiasm clearly shines within these pages, highlighting the achievement each story represents.

We hope you are as pleased with the final selection as we are and that you will continue to enjoy this special collection for many years to come.

CONTENTS

Llanybydder Primary School, Dyfed

Melanie Thomas	74
Aled Davies	76
Fabian Driver	77
Jamie Owen	78
Heledd Thomas	79
Amie Wagner	80
Emma Jones	81
Peter Davies	82
Angharad Evans	83
Meinir Williams	84
Wendy Davies	85
Kelly Jacob	86
Daniella Beaumont	88
Siona Evans	89
Charlotte Murray	90

Monnow Junior School, Newport

Megan Tilley	91
Luke Williams	92
Luke Roberts	93
Jamie Harris	94
Jeremiah Shea	95
Brogan Keepin Davies	96
Danielle Miller	97
Jodie Witch	98
Rhys Davies	99
Chloe Sully	100

Penclawdd Primary School, Swansea

Alex Parkhouse	101
Samuel Devonald	102
Daniel Nurse	103
Daniel Keefe	104
Stephanie Bennett	105
Corey Gunnell	106

Terrace Road Primary School, Swansea

Joshua Dower	141
Dalton Morris	142
Sean Knox	143
Toby Adamson	144
Jessica Hughes	146
Florry Austin	148
Ashleigh Nicholls	149
Rebekah Clement Davies	150
Olivia Head	151
Kirsty Jayne Bell	152
Lloyd Breeze	153
Thomas Adams	154
Grant Wilshere	155
Emily Peters	156
Leah Davey	157
Bilal Miah	158
Steven Van Duinen	159
Carla Wood	160
Emma Rainey	162
Carla James	163
Amir Hussein	164
Joshim Uddin	165
Michael Davis	166

Ysgol Cynlais, Swansea

Lucy Evans	167
Bethany Ellerby	168
Francesca Linton	170
Katrina Klein	172
Anna Lewis	174
Jordan Briskham	176

Ysgol-Y-Castell, Kidwelly

Sophie Smith	177
Rosemary Harris	178
Josi Spiccelli	179
Richard May	180

Ysgol Y Wern, Llanishen

The Stories

THE MIDNIGHT GHOST

One day Lucy invited Fran and Gemma to her house for a sleepover.

That night Gemma said, 'Can you hear a noise coming from the kitchen?'
Lucy and Fran nodded.
Fran said, 'Let's go down and see what it is.'
They tiptoed down the stairs and into the kitchen.

Just then they realised it was someone walking around. Lucy saw a hole in the floor and an eye peeking through.
Lucy said, 'Look over there! There is a hole with an eye looking through it.'

The girls got some flour from the cupboard and lifted three floorboards up and poured the flour into the hole. Then a white figure started sneezing.
Fran said, 'Who are you?'
The white figure said, 'My name is Boo. I live in this hole.'

The next morning they got up and went downstairs with Lucy's mum and dad. When the three girls were eating their breakfast they saw the hole in the floor and the eye. They started to whisper.
Lucy's mum said, 'What are you whispering about?'
They said, 'Nothing.'
They started giggling. Lucy's mum knew they were up to no good by the look on their faces.

Ellie Wikluk (8)
Bwlchgwyn CP School, Wrexham

THE GHOST

One day me and Owen were on our way to the haunted house. It was midnight and when we reached the haunted house doors, a group of bats came flying out.

'Wow!' said Owen.

We suddenly heard this deep moaning voice saying, 'Help me, help me.'

'Maybe we should turn back,' Owen said shakily.

'No, let's go in,' I insisted.

As we walked deeper and deeper into the house the voice got louder and breezier and the floorboards creaked as we sniffed at the horrible smell of rotten cabbage that filled the air. As we entered a room we stopped still.

'Are you drooling on me?' I asked.

'No!' replied Owen.

'Who is then?'

As we looked up we saw a bloodthirsty ghost, with drops of blood hanging from his fangs. Me and Owen were petrified, and rooted to the spot. Suddenly Owen fainted, I tried to scream but I couldn't. I must have fainted too.

When I came round I saw Owen still in a whimpish heap. Then I felt some sticky stuff on my neck. It was blood! Was it mine?

'Ben! Ben! Wake up!'

I opened my bleary eyes to see my mum by my bedside! Thank goodness it had all been a really bad dream.

Ben Salisbury (8)
Bwlchgwyn CP School, Wrexham

A Day In The Life Of A Newborn Lamb

All of a sudden I could see light. I felt something rough underneath me then a warm tongue licking me all over. I could feel something warm and woolly next to me. I turned my head round to see a big white face with big blue eyes. Soon I was dry, I now needed food. I was hungry. But first I had to stand up.

I had four shaky legs. I felt my front two legs bring my body up, then my back. Now there was the problem of finding food. I moved my body so that I could find the teat. I was near it because I could smell the delicious milk.

I drank non-stop with my tail dancing in the air. As soon as I'd had enough to drink I started to look around. I could see other lambs in pens with their mums. There were people filling up buckets and putting hay for the mothers. Some ewes were being moved out of the shed. Where were they going? I hoped that it was somewhere safe with plenty to eat.

Later that day my mum and I were taken out of the shed and into a field. Around me there was plenty of grass. I wanted to play but I didn't want to go too far away from my mum. I decided to jump and prance, keeping an eye all the time on my mum. Soon the sky darkened and I lay by my mother's side. My first day was over.

Emily Williams (9)
Bwlchgwyn CP School, Wrexham

GOING AROUND THE TWIST

One day I went to the fair with my friend Alex. We went to the haunted house. Alex was scared.
I said, 'Come on Alex, nothing will happen.'
So we got in the rusty, rickety cart.

The ride started. We saw a skeleton playing the piano.
I said to Alex, 'Alex, you're quiet.' I turned around and found that Alex had gone! I was worried, my legs turned to jelly.

Suddenly the cart broke down. I heard the rats squealing and the bats. I jumped out of the cart and ran down the rusty track. Then I ran and I ran until I bumped into a ghost with blood-dripping fangs.

I screamed. Suddenly I felt something on my elbow, so I turned around and saw Alex. I said to him, 'Where have you been? I was worried sick.'
'I was caught by that skeleton that was in the piano,' explained Alex.
'Come on let's get out of here,' I said.
We both turned and ran up the track, tripping over the rats as we headed for outside.
'Phew!' I said, 'that was a close shave.'
'I'm never going in there again,' said Alex. We both ran as fast as we could to our homes.

Geraint Edwards (8)
Bwlchgwyn CP School, Wrexham

ONE DAY IN THE LIFE OF A BROWN BEAR

When I first awoke I tried to get off the floor. I could not. I crawled towards my mum who was by the lake. I looked into the water. My reflection was a bear. I had very long claws and brown fur. I saw my mum, she started to lick me. My dad came with some food. It was fish, I started to eat. My surroundings were trees and lakes. My dad was big and strong, my mother was caring and kind.

That afternoon I went out to the lake. I saw a really big fish. I fell in and tried to get out of the water. My legs were too weak. Suddenly my mum came and got me out. I sat on the grass. I looked up at the sky. I stared at the massive white clouds in the sky.

I started to play with my new friends. Suddenly I saw a fox. I started to run. I ran as fast as my legs could carry me. The fox had big gloomy eyes. I looked around, the fox was not there, I was safe. I started to plod along, I felt so alone.

A couple of hours later I found my cave. My mum licked me, my dad took me to the lake. He jumped into the lake and came out with a fish. Now it was my turn. I jumped into the water and came out with a fish. We got to the cave and shared the fish with my mum.

Alex Davies (8)
Bwlchgwyn CP School, Wrexham

THE SPOOKY SLEEPOVER

My name is Gemma, and I was invited to Rebecca's house for a sleepover. She lived in front of a graveyard. We were having something to eat, when we suddenly heard a noise. We ran downstairs.
Rebecca said, 'It's coming from the graveyard.'
I said, 'I don't think we should go to the graveyard.'
But Rebecca was insistent.

When we got outside we could still hear that same noise. As we got closer the noise got louder . . . and louder . . . and louder.
Rebecca said, 'I'll go back and get a torch.'
We crept through the graveyard and we heard a person screaming. We were petrified. We could hardly move.

After a while we felt normal. Just then I said, 'I can see some footprints, let's follow them.'
'OK,' Rebecca said.

We followed the footprints for ages. Suddenly we saw a very old door covered in cobwebs. Rebecca ran to the door and opened it. Inside the room there were skeletons and skulls everywhere. We got so frightened that we ran back to Rebecca's house and we never ever visited graveyards again.

Gemma Nelson (8)
Bwlchgwyn CP School, Wrexham

SPOOKED OUT

One day on a Saturday afternoon me, Ffion and Hatty went to the forest because it was a very sunny day. We didn't realise how long we were there. Night soon fell and we were still in the forest. We noticed suddenly that we couldn't get out!

We heard something rustling in the trees. Ffion and Hatty screamed.
'Help!' I shouted.
'Shh!' whispered something behind us.

It was then that we saw some ghosts right behind us. We noticed they were staring at Hatty's necklace. We couldn't understand why they were interested in the pendant. Hatty remembered that she'd bought the pendant in an antique shop.
'Maybe this necklace belongs to them,' said Hatty.
We heard the ghosts coming back.
'They must be back for the necklace,' we all shouted together.

The ghosts seemed really angry that we had the necklace.
'Hatty just give them the necklace,' I said.
Hatty took off her necklace and left it on the floor. One of the ghosts picked it up.
'Thank goodness they have gone,' we all said.

We followed a path that finally took us out of the forest.
'I'm never going in there again,' said Ffion.
'Neither am I,' I replied.
Hatty was very quiet, but we knew that she too wouldn't be going into the forest again.

Harriet Abbott (8)
Bwlchgwyn CP School, Wrexham

THE VAMPIRE CHASE

I woke up at 7 o'clock and suddenly remembered it was the day me and my friend Ben were going to the fair. I threw my clothes on and went with Mum to pick Ben up. When we got to Ben's house he ran out of the house and got into the car.

When we got to the fair Ben saw a haunted house, 'Let's go in there,' Ben shouted.
It was very spooky. Just then the ghost popped up and scared Ben.
'Ben, it's pretend!' I said.
'Oh,' said Ben.

We travelled more into the house. We came to another door. I opened it and three zombies came howling at us. We ran past them. The next room was full of squealing bats. We closed the door and ran into the next room. We walked in and closed the door.

There was a coffin in there. Ben went up to the coffin and opened it. Ben was petrified for a moment. There was a vampire inside. He woke up and ran after us.

My mum was looking for me and Ben near the roller coaster. We could hear her shouting, 'Owen, Ben, where are you?'
'There's the door,' Ben shouted.
We ran as fast as we could to the door. Luckily the door was open. We ran out to my mum, nearly pushing her over.

Owen Edwards (8)
Bwlchgwyn CP School, Wrexham

A SPOOKY SLEEPOVER

I went to a sleepover at Rebecca's house. Rebecca lived next to a graveyard. It was quite late, but not too late to go out. We heard a moaning voice.

'Why don't we go outside?' suggested Rebecca.

'OK,' I said, 'but I don't want to go anywhere near the graveyard.'

We grabbed our coats and torches and ran outside.

'I triple dare you to go in the graveyard,' Rebecca said.

'OK,' I said daringly.

I played 'tig' with Rebecca around the gravestones.

'See? It isn't that scary after all,' said Rebecca.

A bat flew right past my head and just missed me. I screamed and ran behind Rebecca.

'Now what's the matter?'

'A bat flew past my head,' I replied.

'Oh stop being such a baby.'

We walked a bit further into the graveyard. It was then that I heard a noise. It was a moaning, groaning noise.

'Rebecca, did you hear that noise?' I asked worryingly.

'Yes I did,' said Rebecca who started to quiver.

We saw a moving figure, it was coming closer and closer. We held hands and hid behind the wall. We watched from there. We watched the figure but it was a friendly figure, it was our friend Thomas, he had played a trick on us.

When we went inside we told Rebecca's mum and she said, 'I bet you won't be going out on Hallowe'en night.'

'I bet we will,' said Rebecca smartly.

Francesca Wikluk (8)
Bwlchgwyn CP School, Wrexham

THE GRAVEYARD

One day I went to the graveyard with my mum to put some flowers on my gran's gravestone. After that, my mum went to church and I went to Sunday school. In Sunday school we sang a song and made little boxes with pictures of Jesus on.

When me and my mum got home, we had tea. Later, I went to bed.

I couldn't get to sleep. The howling of the wind was scary. Suddenly I heard a voice, a voice that made me shake and wonder. I went downstairs but my mum wasn't there. I was terrified. Just then I remembered that Mum sometimes went to church in the night. So I put on my clothes and went outside, across the road and into the graveyard. I could not see anything. The sky was pitch-black.

Then I heard the voice again. 'Follow me,' it said.
I began to shake. I went towards the church. But when I opened the door, nobody was there except for an old man. He looked evil. He stood up and gave an evil grin and said, 'So we meet again do we?'
'What do you mean? Where's my mum?' I asked.
'I was going to kill her but she escaped.'

Just then, the vicar appeared. The old man silently went away. I realised that I had been saved by the vicar.

Lucy Thomas (8)
Bwlchgwyn CP School, Wrexham

A LITTLE SCARED

Jack and Caitlin were both eight. They were twins. They only had a dad because their mum had died.

It was Saturday and they were going to the fair. Unfortunately their car broke down on the way there. They stopped next to a big black house. The house had broken windows and had holes in the roof.
'Stay there,' said Dad.
'OK,' they replied.

Dad walked to the front door. The door seemed to open by itself. Dad went inside quietly. 'Hello,' he called out. He thought he heard a voice so he called again, 'Hello.'

Suddenly he saw a ghost. Jack and Caitlin heard their dad scream. He ran out to the car, but he found it empty. Jack and Caitlin had gone. He went back to the house to look for them.

By now he was really worried. 'Jack, Caitlin!' shouted Dad, still worried. He yelled again, 'Jack, Caitlin, come to the car.' But there was no reply. He muttered, 'I'll find the children and then I'll fix the car, then we'll go home!'

So he went to look for the children. He found the children in the end. He fixed the car then they went home.

The next morning they woke up, it had just been a dream.

Chlöe Hudson (8)
Bwlchgwyn CP School, Wrexham

THE TEMPLE OF DOOM

As James was walking through Egypt looking at all the pyramids, he saw a very old one. 'That wasn't there yesterday,' he said.
The pyramid had a sign with its name. It was called *The Temple Of Doom.*

James and his two friends, Tom and Mickey, all went up to the temple.
'Cool,' said James' friends.
They went inside. The doorway was crumbly and cracked.
'Spooky,' said James.
'Shhh!' replied Tom and Mickey together.

They walked down the steep steps. They entered a large room. There were mummy cases all around.
'Did you hear something?' asked James.

Just as he had finished speaking a mummy case opened. A mummy came out and walked towards them. The three boys ran down the steps and found that they couldn't get out!
'We can't escape,' panicked Tom.
'We have to find another way,' said James.
Sand started falling on them. The mummy was getting closer.
'We have to get out now!' said James.

The boys searched for another way out. They entered a passage and found light at the end. They walked towards the light. They pushed stones out of the way so they could get out. The sun dazzled their eyes. They walked to the nearest village but the people there did not believe them when the three boys told them all that had happened. They persuaded their parents to come.

When they got there the pyramid was gone!

Ffion Hammond (7)
Bwlchgwyn CP School, Wrexham

HOW ME AND MY FRIEND BECAME A GHOST!

I had called for my friend Gemma to come for a walk. We were just about to cross the busy main road when we felt a breeze. I had goosebumps on my arms. It didn't seem like anything so we continued.

Then suddenly we felt a gush of wind. Then we heard a car racing fast. We tried to run, to the other side, but we just couldn't as we were rooted to the spot!
'Arrrgggh!' we both screamed.
We then felt a hard blast as the car hit us. We both fell heavily onto the road. Everything went black! That's the last we can remember.

When we woke up we were still on the road. I looked around but somehow it didn't seem the same. I couldn't explain it. The surroundings were the same. I felt for any broken bones but my hand went straight through me! Argh!
'Gemma touch yourself,' I screamed.
Gemma moved her arm but that too went straight through her.
'What's happening?' Gemma whispered shakily.
'I don't know!' I replied with a panic in my voice.

Then we saw our bodies as we floated in the air and people tended to them. But we knew they were too late. Suddenly I realised what we were. We were ghosts.

That's where we are now, living as ghosts, and we will forever.

Rebecca Greenhalgh (8)
Bwlchgwyn CP School, Wrexham

WHY LEAVES ARE GREEN

In the middle of a rainforest, there was a small clearing. In that clearing there stood a small, bedraggled tree. A tree with no life and no hope. Its branches were thin and wiry and the trunk was torn and battered.

One mild autumn day a baby, in a small bamboo cradle, was placed in the tree's branches. The sun grew hotter and hotter as it beat down on the array of brown leaves beneath it.

The tree's roots were sucking up all the water that they could find in the dried up soil. The tree stretched out its branches and shaded the new life that had been laid to rest there.

After a while the baby started to cry for food. It wriggled between the soft bedding and waved its arms around crying for someone to save it.

The tree looked down on the baby, so sweet and innocent, wanting to be loved. The tree shook a succulent fruit from its branches and into the baby's gasping mouth.

That night the baby and the tree slept together under the gleaming heavens above.

Next day the tree woke to find the baby had gone, but the cradle was still there. The tree grasped the cradle and held it close. It was the only thing it had to remember the creature which it had fed the night before.

Many years passed, the tree grew darker and shabbier.
A girl appeared at the tree and said, 'What will you give me now? You gave me your fruit when I was a baby, so what will you give me now?'
'You can have my branches,' said the tree as it looked down on the life it had fed all those years before. 'You can play in them and build a life with them.'

The girl played with the spindly sticks. She had sword fights, clambering in amongst the limbs of the tree. Night came and the girl ran off into the maze of trees. All that was left of the tree was its sturdy trunk and its scattered branches that lay at its feet.

The tree watched day after day, its branches rotted into nothing and it watched its life rot away too.

Many years later a young woman appeared in the small clearing in the woods. 'What will you give me now?' she asked.
'You can have my trunk,' said the tree. 'You can have my trunk and turn it into a canoe and travel around the world, so I can see it too.'

The woman chopped down the trunk and carved out a hole. She set off around the world, taking part of her life with her.

Now, in the small clearing, there stood a wooden stump. A round piece of bark, left, it had been taken by a baby, taken by a girl and taken by a woman.

An old woman turned up at the stump and said, 'What will you give me now?'
'You can have my stump,' said the tree. 'I was there at your beginning and I'm here at your end, tell me your life story.'

So the woman lay down, for the final time, on the stump and she told the tree her life story. And after she did, she died, lying on the provider of her life.

The next day instead of there being a stump in the clearing, there was a beautiful, magnificent tree, with glowing green leaves!

The woman had taken all of the life out of the tree, but in the end she gave her life back, so the tree grew again, but with an extra life, the woman is the green in the leaves.

Nia James (11)
Coed-Y-Lan Primary School, Pontypridd

THE STRANGE OBJECT

'Wake up! Wake up, Mum, Dad, it's my birthday!' shouted Sadie as she jumped on top of her mum and dad's bed.
'OK, we're coming downstairs now,' Sue said.

Off they went downstairs and they all sat down on the sofa in the living room while they watched Sadie open her presents.
'Wow! A set of cars!' said Sadie astonished and pleased.

Her mum and dad had brought her a big set of cars for her birthday, all different colours, and there at the other end, was the biggest, brightest car of all, multicoloured! Sadie asked her parents if she could phone Annabelle to see if she wanted to come and play with her new cars.

Ding-dong. 'Hiya Annabelle, come in and see my brand new set of cars,' Sadie announced proudly.
'Shall we go outside to play?' Annabelle suggested to Sadie.
'Err, yeah OK,' Sadie answered.
The girls gathered the set of cars together and took them outside to play.

All of a sudden, the biggest multicoloured car disappeared and then 10 seconds later appeared again but life-size.
'Argh!' screamed Sadie and Annabelle simultaneously.

The next thing they knew, they found themselves inside the car flying through the air.
'What on earth is going on?' Sadie shouted to Annabelle.
'I don't know!' she shouted back to Sadie.

After a few hours of flying, the girls thought that what they used to think were Sadie's toy cars, were not toy cars at all, they were magical cars.
'Where do you want to go?' the magical car was now speaking to them!
'Cool! How about Australia?'
'Yeah, that sounds OK,' answered the car.

They got to Australia and they landed in a very hot and stuffy jungle.
'Shoot!' shouted Sadie, 'how are we meant to find anything now?'

'I know, we'll get back in the car and ask it to take us somewhere else,' said Annabelle intelligently. They got back in the car but it wouldn't budge.

Meanwhile, back at home, Jake decided he would like to play with one of the cars while Sadie wasn't around to tell him that they were hers and he wasn't allowed to touch them. Just like before, he found himself flying through the air.
'Wow! I don't like this, I feel quite nauseous,' Jake said to himself.

While he was flying around the world he passed Australia, he saw two little dots waving like mad, he thought that he better go down to have a look what was going on. When he got a bit lower down, he could see that it was Sadie and Annabelle.
'Thanks for coming to save us, now put that rope onto this car to pull us because this car won't budge,' Sadie said to the others as her usual bossy self.

They did as Sadie said and they all got home safely, they thought that this would be their little secret.

Sadie Fosterjohn (10)
Coed-Y-Lan Primary School, Pontypridd

SOUR GRAPES

Katy sat on the bench in the park with her friends.

'I'm getting a mobile phone for my birthday,' Sarah told Katy and Carys.

'So am I. I'm getting a Nokia and my dad is getting it for me next week. It is so cool,' Carys sounded really excited.

'Great! I can phone you. Are you getting a mobile Katy?' Sarah asked.

'No. My mum and dad think they are a waste of time. My dad keeps saying to use the house phone.'

'That's bad. Why can't you just pretend you want it for emergencies?' Carys asked.

'I don't really want one,' Katy replied.

When Katy got home she went to find her mum. 'Mum!'

'I'm upstairs,' her mother called.

'Mum, can I have a mobile phone?'

'We've already been through this Katy.'

'But Mum, I could have it for an emergency. What if I need to call you when I'm out with my friends? Please Mum! I really want one!'

'OK, I'll speak to your dad about it and maybe you can have one.'

'Yes! Thanks Mum, you're the best.'

It wasn't long before her dad came home from work. Katy sneaked downstairs to listen to what her mum and dad were saying.

'Well I suppose if she needed it to call us from somewhere . . .' Katy could hear her dad talking.

Katy decided to walk into the room. 'Hello Dad.'

'We've decided you can have a mobile Katy. I'm going to get it now.'

'Can I come too? Can I go with you Dad?'

'No. It's a surprise.' Katy's dad left to get the mobile.

When he came back Katy went to open the box which he held.

'It's the wrong one,' Katy shouted at the mobile in the box.

'I thought you would like this one,' Katy's dad said.

'I suppose it doesn't matter. I didn't really want one that much,' Katy left her mobile on the table and went upstairs.

Clare Allen (10)
Coed-Y-Lan Primary School, Pontypridd

ROUNDER BALL

When the doorbell rings at three in the morning it's never good news.

Alex Rider was woken by the first chime. His eyes flickered open but for a moment he stayed completely still in his bed, lying on his back with his head resting on his pillow. He heard a bedroom door open and a creak of wood as somebody went downstairs. The bell rang a second time and he looked at the alarm clock showing beside him 3.02am. There was a rattle as someone slid the security chain off the front door.

He rolled out of bed and walked to the open window, his bare feet pressing down on the carpet pile. The moonlight spilled onto his chest and shoulders. As he looked out he saw about half a dozen black cars parked outside his house. He crawled out of his bedroom window onto his porch roof.

With a bang the two men walked out quite seriously so Alex followed them, but as soon as Alex got behind them they turned and said, 'Hey! What's your name?'
Alex replied, 'My name is Alex Rider.'
One of them asked Alex, 'Is Ian Rider your father?'
Alex replied, 'No he is my uncle.'
The other one whispered, 'Follow me but tell your mother first.'
Alex just went to the living room and went to the kitchen to follow them into a tinted-windowed Mercedes-Benz. He fell asleep.

Alex was woken by a tedious, 'Alex! Alex! are you awake?' Then a Russian voice whispered, 'I will kill you. I'll put the mysterious Rounder Ball in your mouth.'

While Alex was asleep some strange green slime came of his mouth turning blue, yellow and finally red.

Suddenly a South African voice said, 'Take him to hospital. He is ill, can't you see?' So then he was carried into a Y reg Vauxhall Astra van with a driver and a passenger.

After a while the van stopped just before the hospital and the driver said, 'There's no point in going to hospital. I am Herod Sayle, I am a contract plumber.' Then a gun fired and Alex dropped. 'I mean a killer, aren't I?

Phillip Cullen (10)
Fairfield Primary School, Penarth

A FUNNY FAIRY TALE

Once there was a really, really handsome prince in love with a really, really poor peasant girl, but the peasant was really, really lovely.

One day Pearl and Leo (because that was their names) were in the middle of a really big kiss, when Leo was sent a letter that read, 'The king is on his deathbed so come and see him, he is your father after all'. So off Leo went. *Clipperty-clop, clipperty-clop.*
'Oh here's the castle.' So in Leo went, up the stairs and because the stairs were so big he had to make base camp on the stairs. In the morning Leo went up to this dad's deathbed.
'I want you to get married,' said the king.
'Oh, oh good,' said Leo.
'Yeah, to Princess Smelly Sock, daughter of King Lost His Marbles.'
And with that the king died, *bonk!*
And because it's always polite to do something for someone on his or her deathbed Leo sent a letter to Smelly Sock but King Lost His Marbles replied. 'She has to marry you because I'm King Cuckoo Cuckoo Raaassspp.'

Well Smelly Sock would have preferred to stay home and read a good book until she croaked it. When Leo and Smelly Sock were about to marry a messenger burst in and told everyone King Lost His Marbles had been squished by an elephant while swimming in Africa but he swam in sand not water. So Leo and Smelly Sock didn't have to get married, so Smelly Sock ran home to her books that King Lost His Marbles had eaten before he went to Africa.

Leo saw the messenger was Pearl and they got married and lived happily ever after.

Oliver Morgan (10)
Fairfield Primary School, Penarth

MYSTERY PLUG

One Saturday morning me, Grant and Craig went swimming. Grant spluttered, 'Watch me dive.' He noticed a heavy chain as his head popped above the water. He whispered, 'I've found something.' I put my goggles on and dived in with Craig.

Craig and I then found it. We all gripped it and pulled, it caused a whirlpool. One by one people got sucked in with the water, some people were sucked all the way to Hong Kong, Ibiza and a lot of other places.

Afterwards the Navy had to try to refill the pool and put the plug back in.

Josh Tyler (11)
Fairfield Primary School, Penarth

The Land Of Dinosaurs

One night two sneaky kids called Lee Bezant and Josh Tyler were in their school lab looking at an invention some nerd had made. There was a letter by the invention, it said, 'Don't touch', but the boys ignored it and pressed the red button.

It sucked them in and took them back to 65,000,000 BC: The dinosaur age. Lee and Josh had landed in a massive forest which didn't look very friendly. 'This doesn't look very friendly,' said Josh.
'Where are we?' Lee said.
'I have no idea.'
'I think we've gone back in time to when the dinosaurs lived,' said Lee.
'We can't have,' said the two boys.
Then they heard something which sounded very big.
'Uh oh,' said Lee.
'Let's run,' said Josh.
'No,' Lee said, 'we should hide.'
'How do you know?' said Josh.
'Because I do! That's how.'

The two boys jumped under a fallen tree trunk and a T-rex ran straight past them but it stopped about 100 yards away and turned around and charged right back at them.

Luck had stuck with them and an allosaurus jumped out and attacked the T-rex. The sound of the T-rex's cry was so loud it sent them back to the present.

They both had a scar on their arms like a sword had been pushed through their arm or a needle gouged through. To them it was a mystery they never remembered or understood.

Lee Bezant (11)
Fairfield Primary School, Penarth

Pass It On

One day a little girl called Janet was out to do the shopping in town because her mother was ill. On the shopping list was beans, bacon, sausages and some eggs. When she had got all of that she set off home. She saw an old lady on the way who was her next-door neighbour and was carrying a heavy basket. Janet offered to take it home for the old lady and she was allowed to.

When Janet went back to her house the old lady said she must have a reward, but Janet said, 'No, I don't want a reward, just pass my kindness on.'

The next day the old lady she went on a bus to the seaside. Just as the bus was going to start the old lady spotted a boy with no money. She remembered Janet's words, *'Just pass my kindness on'*, so the old lady gave the boy some money and the lady said to pass it on too!

The boy's father was so pleased with the old lady he built a big park in town and that passed kindness on to everyone.

Callum Blunt (8)
Fairfield Primary School, Penarth

A Day In The Life Of My Mum!

I woke up to the sun filtering through the curtains, struggling to reach me. I struggled to get back to sleep but it was too late Steve had already brought my cup of tea through and Catherine was bouncing up and down on my bed excited that she was going swimming with the school this morning.

Steve dropped Catherine to school so I was soon on my own. I saw a cobweb so I couldn't help but get my duster and sweep it away.

Then I emptied the washing basket into the washing machine and then slipped into some suitable clothes to go down to Steve's site and drop off his sandwiches for lunch. I did this and then went to the dry cleaners to drop off some suits. They said it would be done by tomorrow.

I slipped away from the dry cleaners and then went and did my weekly shopping and there were more things for Catherine than anyone.

It was soon the end of the day so I picked up Catherine and her friend Naomi from school and then they went and played upstairs experimenting with make-up or something.

We had pizza for tea, well not me I had salad since I'm on a diet like always. I got a bit tired after that so I slipped into bed and then read for a while and then thought to myself, *being me isn't so bad, I have a life I'm pleased with.*

Catherine Salvidge (10)
Fairfield Primary School, Penarth

THE GHOST THAT LIVES IN MY CUPBOARD

Today we moved into a new house, I didn't know my way around yet, but I'm sure I will soon. My dad has just put my bed up, so I can sleep in it tonight.

'Goodnight Dad,' I said to him.

'Goodnight.'

As I got into my bed I heard this rumbling noise coming from my cupboard, but I ignored it, but then it started getting louder so I stuck my head under my pillow.

The wind whistled loudly smacking a tree's branch on my window. My head came out from under the pillow, I got out of bed and walked to the mirror. I looked behind me and saw a white pale face in the bedroom. I ran back to my bed and saw my cupboard slam.

A voice said, 'Come to the cupboard, where am I, I am over there, look in the cupboard.' I walked over to my cupboard and put my hand on the cold handle and I opened it and *'Boo!'*

I fell to the floor but I never woke up. I, I . . . I think I am never going to wake up.

Sophie Wright (11)
Fairfield Primary School, Penarth

A Spooky Graveyard

It was a cold winter's night when Summer went to visit her mother's grave. She was standing in the field thinking of her mum when the doors of the church started to slam.

She went over to the doors to see what was there but all she found was a rope hanging from the ceiling with a dummy hanging inside.

She screamed and ran to her car but the car was not there so she looked around the block and found the car in a driveway. She started the car up and drove for a few minutes when she heard a mumbling noise so she stopped the car to see what it was and she saw a sheet moving about.

She ran to the phone booth and phoned for a cab. The ride came within three minutes and she got in the cab and said, 'Can you take me to Saundersfoot?' but the man turned and laughed. He had crooked teeth and big frizzy hair which made her scream so she said, 'I'll pass, thanks,' and got out of the car and started to run home when the crazy driver started to chase her.

She charged through a smoky lane when she heard a voice that said, 'You're not safe anywhere,' so she sprinted home and banged on the door but to her surprise nobody was in and she looked in the window and saw a shadow in the window with big frizzy hair.

Faye Harper (11)
Fairfield Primary School, Penarth

A DAY IN THE LIFE OF DAVID BECKHAM

It was 7am in the Beckham household. All was silent. *Beep, beep, beep, beep,* David's alarm went off. It was the day of the FA Cup Finals. The England team had made it.

He put the shower on. He got in. In one hour he was out and changed. He changed into his brand new England shirt. The phone rang, it was Ryan Giggs. This was their telephone conversation . . .
'Alright David?'
'Alright Giggs?'
'Yeah, I am alright, oh good luck in the match.'
'Oh thanks.'
'Bye.'
'Bye.'
Beeeeep. That was the end of the phone conversation.

It was 9am in no time. He had to get to the Millennium Stadium. The black car with tinted windows pulled up to take David Beckham.

He pulled up, thousands of fans stood there screaming. People of all ages stood there with pieces of paper for him to sign and banners saying, *I Love You David* and other ways to trying and catch David's attention.

In no time at all the match had begun. Within fifty minutes David had scored twice. From the Brazilian side, they had scored once. The whistle blew. *England had won.*

Laura Kennedy (11)
Fairfield Primary School, Penarth

A Day In The Life Of A Victorian Servant

Hello, I'm awake at 5am to do my orders before the cook comes because she gets so mad when I haven't got the food ready.

I go off to do the cleaning around the fireplace. I need to get the gold polisher and cloth from the kitchen cupboard.

Now I am scrubbing the gold fireplace as hard as I can to get it cleaned so the master will be pleased.

I'm now on to chopping up the food before cook comes.

I've now got to get nice and tidy to answer the door because master likes me nice and tidy when guests arrive for dinner.

Here I am at dinner time with all the guests sitting at the table. I am now taking the food and *splat* all of the food went over my master.
The master stood up and shouted, 'You crackpot Gareth Thomas! That's it, you're not having any leftovers or money for three days.'
'OK.'

There's nothing to do now so I may as well go to sleep, but after I do the washing and hang it out.

Bye! Goodnight for now.

Nathan Jones (11)
Fairfield Primary School, Penarth

BEHIND THE TRAPDOOR

I hate school, every day I get bullied, I know why, I'm poor. My dad left when my mum was pregnant with me, he didn't want children. Now my mum works in a foul bar which is full of drunken men.

Now I'm in Year 7 I'm still being bullied. It's a Year 10 girl called Trixsey who's pretty and fashionable, I'm normal and tatty.

When I got home my mum was making eggs. I love my mum but she's always out late. She was wearing jeans, a blue top and her brown hair was in a ponytail.

After tea I went to bed. I looked at the trapdoor in the corner of the bedroom. It doesn't open but I believe behind it is a better life for me, a posh house and a ballet house for me to dance in. I'm dreaming. I want to be there.

'Cushet.' It's time to go to school.
As I walked through the gate Trixsey approached.
'Well if it isn't Cushet, it looks like you live in a bin! Oh hang on - you do!'
I turn to walk away but she kept going. 'Hey Cushet! Mum been arrested yet?' She knew she'd hit home and I cried.

When I went to bed I tried to open the trapdoor but it wouldn't open, so I kicked it. A tiny piece of wood flew up, I reached in and pulled the trapdoor open.

There was nothing, just a brick wall, no better life for me. Nothing behind the trapdoor.

Jenny Grant (11)
Fairfield Primary School, Penarth

A DAY IN THE LIFE OF A VILLAIN

10am
I wake up in The Designator, my evil lair where I plan world domination. Fluffy my cat with mind reading powers is chasing his tail. Sometimes I think I'd be better with a man-eating iguana.

11am
I eat my breakfast of Clown Os and have thought of a plan to conquer the world. I will dump nuclear waste into the sea and set killer rodents loose. I will fly in a plane which will explode the Sphinx.

11.30am
The workers are dead, I shot them for insolence. I asked for coffee and they brought me tea. Who shall I depend on now? My Gungan army could be useful.

11.45am
My Gungan army is ready having been armed with Schimitars which are spear-swords and voltage shields and also a few other gadgets to kill the President of the United States.

12.10am
My army is ready, it is marching towards the USA, this could take all day. Ha, ha, ha, ha, ha!

4pm
I am so angry, can hardly write - Professor Derneritor took over the world before me. I blasted him into the ocean afterwards. People are calling me a hero. What's the commotion?

6pm
After drowning Fluffy in my swamp I bought an iguana. I will call him Chameleon. He is a rare iguana that can change colour.

8pm
Chameleon uses his little death ray, already he has blasted 6 flies, I'm so proud of him. Trying to plot villainous schemes has been unsuccessful. I curse all my enemies.

9pm

After watching my favourite TV show, 'World Domination Isn't Everything It Is The Only Thing' and feeding Chameleon. I retired to my quarters to read 'Villains Through The Ages' by Morgane Le Faye. I went to bed, tomorrow is a good day for world conquest. Ha, ha, ha, ha!

Jordan Lloyd (11)
Fairfield Primary School, Penarth

THE HAUNTED HOUSE

One morning Holly was looking in the paper and said, 'Let's go and look at the house on the hill.'
'Yeah, that sounds great,' said Chloe.
When they had had their breakfast all three of them set off.

'It looks creepy, let's go home,' whispered Zoe, (she's the youngest).
'No,' shouted the other two.
So they went in and looked around.
'Boo, boo!'
'Stop trying to scare us Zoe,' they said.
'It wasn't me.'

Suddenly a crash and a bang, it went dark, the candle went out and a trapdoor opened. They screamed for help.
'Boo, boo.'
'Stop yelling,' said Chloe.
Then they saw a . . . ghost and a monster.
'Run!' they yelled.

Zoe and Chloe never went there again, but Holly wanted to stay and make friends.
'Are you nuts?' shouted Chloe.
'Leave here,' said Zoe.
'I am going back,' shouted Holly. So off Holly went up to the very top, she could see her town up there. All of a sudden she fell all the way down. She broke her leg and the monster came. She tried to run but it was too late.

When Holly didn't come home the others rang 999 and the policeman said, 'I am sorry, you will never see your sister alive again.'

Zoe and Chloe were very upset for a long time.

Jessica Grant (10)
Fairfield Primary School, Penarth

DESTROYER VS OLIVER

The mad scientist James was very busy. He was making a destroyer, it would be the most powerful thing on Earth. It had the strength of 100 bulls and the speed of 201 Ferraris. The machine also had very powerful balls that could destroy a continent in half an hour, and the whole universe in a year (not including the time it takes to get into space). It could fly around the Earth in 60 days. 'Ha, ha, ha, ha, ha!' laughed the evil genius.

'It is a very cool machine Sir,' said Rhys with a cold stare at the machine.

'I have to say it is quite a machine,' replied James, 'Destroyer couldn't be any more perfect.'

It was a perfect fighting machine but then it suddenly destroyed the lab before flying up into the sky and destroying every living thing on Earth!

It then went to Hong Kong and destroyed every bit of land, then it went to Africa but in China there was a boy who actually survived, his name was Diver. He knew what had happened to the robot. It was programmed to destroy the entire universe. The young warrior went to fight the destroyer. When he got to it they had an indescribable battle. They destroyed the world including themselves. No one forgot the warrior, some people said he was foolish.

Genius Khumalo (10)
Fairfield Primary School, Penarth

THE BULLY

Alex was walking to school and then saw Zack the big bully. Zack pushed him over and took his money for tuck and ran off. When Alex got up he'd hurt himself.

His mum got out of the car and said, 'What happened?'

'A boy pushed me over and took my money.'

When he got to school he saw his friends Phillip and Oliver so he went over to see them but Zack and his gang stopped him.

Zack said, 'Give me your lunch, now!'

Alex tried to run away from them but Zack pulled his lunch bag off him and ran off with his lunch. When he went upstairs he told Miss Morgan, Zack had to stay in school another hour.

After school Alex went home and phoned Oliver. When Oliver came over he told Oliver something then Oliver went away. Oliver went to his classmates' houses and told them to meet him at the park. They were thinking of a plan to get back at Zack.

Zack was still in school and when he got out of school he went to a boarded up house where Alex set a trap. When he got to the house with his friends, Alex went out of the house and then ran inside. Zack chased after him until a net was dropped onto him. The bully was defeated.

James Brown (10)
Fairfield Primary School, Penarth

ONE DAY IN THE LIFE OF MYSELF

One day, a very long time ago Ruby and her brother found a very small spaceship. Her brother touched the small spaceship and it went bigger. A long door opened and she said to her brother, 'There are lots of strange things, come and see.'
'OK,' said Matteus. Then Matteus walked up the long door. When Matteus got in the long door closed.
'I'm scared Matteus,' said Ruby.
'Don't worry, at least we're together,' cried Matteus.

They then came to a stop and Ruby and Matteus dropped out of the spaceship. They found themselves in a jungle.
'We're in a jungle,' said Ruby. 'Look there's a lion, let's go and stroke it.'
'No, they're dangerous,' said Matteus.
Ruby and Matteus went more and more into the jungle. Ruby got more and more scared. Matteus said, 'It's going to be OK now.'
'No, it's not!' said Ruby. Ruby meant that there was a herd of elephants running at them.

Ruby and Matteus could talk to animals and Ruby started to talk to the tigers. To the lions she said, 'Can you help us find our way home?'
'Yes,' said the lion.
'Do you like us?' said the kangaroo.
The tiger said, 'Let's go take you to the sea. We'll take you to the boat, come on, let's go!'
'OK.'
'Do you want a ride?'
'Yes please,' said Matteus and Ruby. 'Hey look there's a helicopter, let's go home now.'

Matteus and Ruby had a brilliant time.

Ruby Angove (10)
Fairfield Primary School, Penarth

CRAZY GOLF

One day Steve and Henry were having a delightful walk in the forest in Devon. The sun was blazing down on them through the trees. Their walk was interrupted by some noise beaming round the forest. Steve and Henry had to go and look what was happening. They peered through the trees and saw a building site.
'I wonder who's under this?' Henry said.
'Look carefully,' Steve said.

Henry looked carefully but he still couldn't see anything. Steve pointed to a man in a black suit with an evil smirk and messy black hair. It was Dr Vile. He was building a crazy golf course on Devon Common!

Crash! A tree fell down inches away from Henry. 'Run!' yelled Steve. They both ran straight on. *Crash!* Another tree came down. They hurdled over the trees.

When they got home they thought the sound of a golf course was quite a good idea.

Isaac Minns (9)
Fairfield Primary School, Penarth

THE HOUSE

One bright sunny morning Mr Morris was walking down his road when suddenly a dark, gloomy house caught his eye. He turned and saw what only looked like a ruined house still in use. Mr Morris looked through the doorway very quietly and saw a lady coming. Mr Morris quickly ran away thinking that it was creepy.

The next morning Mr Morris went to see Dr Edwards and told her all about the creepy house and they both decided to check the house out in the night to see if anything strange would happen.

That night Dr Edwards and Mr Morris walked down the road and all of a sudden stopped in shock only to see that the lady was flying in the sky. That could only mean one thing - she was a witch. Mr Morris and Dr Edwards quickly ran back home and went to bed like nothing had happened.

The next day they knew that they needed to tell the police because they knew that witchcraft was forbidden so they went to the police station to put her in jail. The police turned up on her doorstep and arrested her for witchcraft.

Craig Warner (11)
Fairfield Primary School, Penarth

V2

Joe, the cloud Shyro, was walking around his home when he saw a speedy pida bus. Don't ask! These were just rare! So he decided to hop on. 'One ticket to Virtustation please!' said Joe.

The bus was dark and gloomy, but Joe found his way around. Soon they were there and the bus came to a halt.
'Vstation stop, please watch yer step and have a nice day. Next stop, Krawk island,' said the bus driver, sounding like he had just had an electric shock.

The Vstation was a big place. The inside walls were silver and red all over. Joe was feeling hungry, so he went to the café and had a snack.
'Hello, how can I help you?' said the Vstation manager.
'Hi, I'd like to book a hotel room, please,' said Joe casually with a small yawn.
'Ah, let's see now. You can - ooh, you can have the top room!'
'Thanks!' said Joe taking the key from him.

He found an empty elevator and took it to the top floor. *Ping!* went the door, but it didn't open. Instead it whooshed to the bottom floor. *Crash!* A small box hit the floor and turned on.
'I'm V2,' said the box.
'V what?' said Joe.
'V2. One of Doctor Sloth's inventions. Let's play a game called Kalora's Kaus!' said V2.
'I haven't got time for baby games! Let me out please,' asked Joe nicely. But as he took a step forward, a zap of electricity just missed him. 'Or maybe I could stay for a bit,' he said, taking a step backwards.

Joe grew weary of the game, but he couldn't do anything about it! He had been in there for two days until he finally plucked up the courage to pull his plug. As he pulled it, he went berserk with an electric shock.

Ping! went the lift as it opened. He went to the manager to complain and got a lifetime membership. He stayed the night and then went home.

Joe was walking around his house when he saw a speedy pida bus. *Slam!* went the door.
'To the desert, please!' said Joe.

Jordan Ford (10)
Fairfield Primary School, Penarth

THE WACKY WIZARD

In a castle far away, the wizard of laughter was casting a spell to have lots of gold, but first he got a cat of scare. He tried three more times but he got a mouse of run master. They both made friends with the wizard of laughter, but they did not make friends with each other.

They chased each other round the castle. As they were chasing each other, they saw some strange and funny things. They also saw something they had never seen before. It was a television. They were amazed for a minute and said it was just like them, but their names were Tom and Jerry. As they were watching, they made friends again and had a game of touch. They enjoyed it and the wizard, cat and mouse lived very happily together.

Danielle Allen (10)
Fairfield Primary School, Penarth

THE BIG MATCH

They had done it - they had got to the final of the Future Footballers' Cup and they were playing their sworn rivals, Twoafan Primary. They beat St John's 7-0 to get to the final.

Rex and Tony were walking down the corridor when they bumped into Mr Pugh, the gym teacher. He said, 'You should be proud of yourselves. You've made it to the team.'
There was a rush of joy as they jumped up and down, then sensibly Rex said, 'Where are we playing, Sir?'
'We are playing at Ninian Park,' he answered. He also announced that Travis McBerd was playing for Twoafan.

The whistle blew and the crowd chanted as Twoafan dominated possession. They passed the ball to Travis who span away from his defender and powered a terrifying shot, only to be stopped by an acrobatic save from Tony. Travis ran down the wing, cut back inside and found himself running into the box. Tony did an awful dive, the referee gave a penalty and they scored.

In the second half things were looking better for Middleton. James Parkinson whipped a cross in only to be headed over the bar. Suddenly Rex saw a gap, called for the ball, sprinted through the gap, shot and scored. With two minutes left, Tony jogged up into the box. The ball curled in and Tony put in a powerful header. The whistle blew. They were going crazy, they just could not get over it, they had beaten their rivals Twoafan. They lifted the trophy and fireworks sprouted out from behind them.

When they returned to school the following morning, they had a special assembly and they lifted the trophy again.
The Principal said, 'But the real credit has to go to Tony who scored the winning goal. So let's give him a clap.'
After that they gave the team three cheers, 'Hip hip hooray, hip hip hooray!'

Joshua Hurley (10)
Fairfield Primary School, Penarth

THE WHISPERER

Alice looked out of the window and stared at the front lawn as a hot light shone through onto the window sill, which made her move. Once more she had heard the voice. 'Alice, don't be afraid,' whispered a sweet, soft voice.

She went outside, thinking it was all in her head an then spotted her dad talking to some guests. She waited in the long grass for him to finish telling his favourite joke. She felt a tap on her shoulder and turned round to see another girl, but she had a pale face and a white dress. She didn't look like a normal girl.

'Argh!' screamed Alice.

'Alice,' said her dad, 'what's the matter?'

'It's that girl, Dad. She's a g-g-ghost!' Alice answered.

'Which girl?' asked her dad.

Alice turned round and the girl wasn't there.

Later on, Alice was in bed when she heard the voice again. 'Please don't be afraid. I just want to . . .'

'Who are you?' Alice yelled as she jumped out of bed. 'What do you want?'

At that moment her mum came into the room. 'Calm down, Alice, and go to sleep,' she muttered as she walked out.

'I just want to tell you something might happen to you,' said the voice.

She saw the girl in the mirror and as she went to speak to her, she disappeared.

Maybe she was trying to tell Alice something important - something very important.

Amy Evans (10)
Fairfield Primary School, Penarth

A LIFE IN HELL

One day Laura went downstairs and took the dolls upstairs. She put the Indians in the doll's house, then opened the back of the doll's house to put in some dolls she had found under her bed. Suddenly, all of the Indians had disappeared. Laura cried and thought about them as she tried to go to sleep.

The next day when the alarm went off, Laura got up and went to check if the dolls were there and if the Indians had come back. She was shaking as she slowly opened the door of the doll's house. It creaked really loudly and then Laura smelt smoke. She shouted out loud, 'Help! Oh, help!' but no one could hear her.
Then Strawberry came along. He was one of the Indians.
'Who are you?' asked Laura.
'My name is Strawberry. I was an Indian.'
'Well, can you get me out of here, Strawberry?'
'Yes, but you have to pass the test.'
'Do I have to?'
'Well, if you want to get out, then yes you do!'
Strawberry and Laura walked over the hot rocks and then fell through a hole. They both got out but Strawberry was not supposed to turn into a human. Suddenly, they fell through a hole.

Two years later, Laura was crying when Strawberry popped out of nowhere.
'What is the matter, Laura?' Strawberry said.
'We are in Hell and the Devil was trying to kill me, so I cried.' Laura had remembered that if he cried her love would come back. Laura went to strangle the Devil and remembered the Devil would die if she made love to someone, so she snogged Strawberry. Hell died and Strawberry had turned into a doll. Laura remained a human and hopefully would live normally from now on.

Laura Bone (11)
Fairfield Primary School, Penarth

PENGUIN POWER

Mandy rushed through the driveway of her house as the horn of a car beeped. As she got closer to the car, a face peeped out.

'Hi Mandy,' said the face.

Mandy suddenly remembered who it was. 'Lilly,' shouted Mandy, 'oh, it's so good to see you.'

'You too,' replied Lilly.

Lilly was Mandy's best friend but she had to move away with her grandfather because her mum and dad couldn't look after her.

'Enough talking, climb in so we can go,' said Lilly's grandfather.

They set off.

Lilly's grandfather had a ship and he had promised Mandy he would take her there one day. This was the day!

Lilly's grandfather was taking the girls on a tour of the Antarctic Ocean.

It didn't take long to actually get there because Mandy lived in Churchill, a frosted town with icicles hanging on the roofs. At last they were on the ship sailing in the ocean. As Lilly's grandfather was explaining about the penguins, Mandy noticed something black in the water.

'Oil,' she shouted, 'there's oil in the water.'

Lilly ran over. 'But people on shore will die if it's poisonous.'

'Never mind about that,' said Lilly's grandfather, 'what about the penguins? They are already rare in Churchill.'

'Oh, we've got to save them,' said Mandy.

But it was too late. The penguins had swum into the thick, black oil.

'Swim out, swim out,' said Lilly.

Then something happened. The penguins dived under the water and disappeared. Then Mandy felt something touch her back. She looked round and saw a whole pile of black and white splodges, hundreds of them.

'The penguins,' she cried, 'they really have power.'

Bethan Savory (9)
Fairfield Primary School, Penarth

THE BIG WAVE

Up the wave, up, nearly, bailed.
Eddie felt the water on his face as he fell. He had failed the big wave again!

As he walked home, dejected, he saw a shiny board in a shop. It was a short board, just what he needed to ride the big wave! But then he saw the price! £300! How could he afford that? He only had £210 and it would take ages to save up the extra £90. Then he had an idea.

When he got to the beach he saw Gordo straight away. He was so tall, he was hard to miss! He ran up to him. 'Hey, Gordo, I've got this problem. I need to buy this board and it costs £300. So can I, er, borrow £90?' Eddie gabbled.
'Only if I can see you ride the big wave!' Gordo replied.
Eddie was shocked, but he agreed. 'Deal,' he said.
Gordo gave him the money. Eddie went off home, picked up the rest of the money, went to the shop and bought the board. Feeling happy, he strolled home, but as he got nearer to his house he began to feel uneasy. What if he couldn't do it?
'What's the matter, dear?' said Eddie's mum.
Eddie explained and his mum said, 'All you need is confidence.'
She's right, Eddie thought.

The next day Eddie went straight to the beach. Gordo was waiting.
'Well, here I go,' said Eddie.
Up, up, *yes!* He did it!
'Yes!' he shouted. He realised it hadn't been his board. It was his confidence! He'd wasted his money! 'Well, I needed a new board!' laughed Eddie.

Owen Davies (9)
Fairfield Primary School, Penarth

A Trip To The Antarctic

Peter and Alice were two of the best travellers in Britain.

One day they were sitting at home when the phone rang. Alice got out of her chair to answer it. Five minutes later she went back into the living room with a big smile on her face. Peter got up, went to Alice and asked her who was on the phone. They both sat down and Alice told him everything.

About fifteen minutes later, they were packing their bags to leave for the Antarctic. That's what the phone call was about.

The next day they were on a ship to go to Antarctica. Two months later they were there on the cold, frozen ice, ready to take some chances on the cold - no freezing, land. Peter was an excellent fisher so they could have fish for tea, cooked on their little stove.

A day later they were ready to dive and see all the fish. They saw over twenty different fish and also saw some seals and lots of penguins. As soon as they were on the ice, they knew something had changed and they knew what. The temperature had dropped and it was a lot colder than before. They had only been on the ice for three days, but if they were not home in twenty-four hours they might not survive.

Peter got the emergency radio and asked for a helicopter. They did not know that it would take four days to get back home by helicopter, but at least they would be warm.

Four days later they were taken to hospital to be checked over. It would be a while before they would go there again.

Hannah Rose Bedford (10)
Fairfield Primary School, Penarth

IT'S ALIVE!

We had just finished unpacking so we decided to go and explore. I had just turned 16 and this was my first holiday without parents.

'Let's go and see the pyramids,' said Kim.

We took some water and off we went.

When we got there, there were bars around the pyramids.

A guard said, 'Sorry kids, these pyramids are closed. It's not safe anymore. Now go and stay out of trouble.' He shoved us off.

'Now what are we going to do?' screamed Kim in a bad mood. *'Argh!'* she screamed as she fell through a hole.

'Argh,' I screamed as I followed her.

We landed in a heap on the floor of a strange room. The smell of the dust was horrible. I stood up and got my torch out of my bag. I switched it on and soon realised which room we were in.

'Kim, we're in the burial chamber.'

Thump! Chloe had fallen through the hole too. I shone my torch on a mummy case. The lid was moving! I turned to Kim and Chloe, then back to the case. The mummy was crawling out!

We screamed and then a rope ladder appeared at the hole. We climbed up quickly with Chloe at the bottom. The mummy tried following us, but Chloe kicked it back down. We quickly scrambled up into the open air.

'I think it's going to be a long time before I go on holiday again!' I said.

'Me too,' said Chloe as we walked into the sunset.

Rachel McCulloch (10)
Fairfield Primary School, Penarth

THE LOST WORLD 2

Sarah's boyfriend, Paul, had a row with John Hammond about sending her to Isla Sorna with dinosaurs which John had created.

Paul went to Isla Sorna with a group to look for Sarah. They found her easily when she scared Nick (one of the members) and he nearly fell off the log he was standing on. Paul just stood there with Sarah's lucky backpack and said, 'Have you been attacked?'
'No, that's how it always looks,' she replied.
The group carried on through the wood until they came to a stop.
'Sarah, no! Stop! Wait!'
Sarah had gone to see the stegosaurus herd feeding when she came to a baby stegosaurus feeding on leaves. She slowly approached and took a picture.
Paul started to worry, saying, 'You can't touch it. Don't get so close.'
Sarah took one last picture and then her film ran out. The baby gave a roar and the herd got angry.
'They're just protecting their baby,' said one of the group.
Paul said, 'So am I.'
Sarah got in the middle and one stegosaurus started to chase her. She hid in a log, but one of the dinosaur's spikes went through it.
When Sarah came out, the dinosaurs had gone.

The group carried on until they came out into the open and then danger appeared.
The next book will tell you what danger they faced.

Jacques Duval (10)
Fairfield Primary School, Penarth

THE SPIDER

The silence on Strawberry Hill that morning was broken by loud barks, miaows and squeaks from (as you have probably guessed) three particular animals.

'I'm the most important on Strawberry Hill,' barked Spot.

'No, I am,' miaowed Socks.

'I'm pretty sure that I'm the most important,' came a small, weak but certain voice from Sticks (who was hiding beneath their feet).

'Look, since we all think we're so important, why don't we go and ask the owl in the willow tree?' suggested Spot.

'Good idea,' said Socks.

'Good idea,' echoed Sticks.

The owl was the wisest animal on Strawberry Hill. He lived in a small, bent willow tree at the bottom of Strawberry Hill and had the answer to everybody's problems.

'Um, excuse me,' said Sticks in the tiniest voice. 'Um, we were wondering if you could tell us who is the most important animal here?'

'None of *you*, that's for sure! The most important animal here is the spider.'

'The spider?' shouted everyone.

'Yes. The animal who eats all the flies and insects which are harmful to man's crops. If there were no spiders, there would be no food for us to eat and eventually, one by one, we would all die of starvation and flies and bugs would rule the world.'

'I guess that we should be thankful for all that the spider has done then,' said the animals.

Afterwards, the whole of Strawberry Hill had a celebration in honour of the spider. They all lived happily together without arguing, thanks to the owl and the spider.

Amelia Macey (10)
Fairfield Primary School, Penarth

HOBO STRIKES RICH

It was another agonising night awake for Joe. He was a homeless man who bought drugs off dealers to end his life. He wore a pair of dirty trousers, second-hand, food-stained jacket and top hat. He had mousy grey hair and a bristly beard.

Joe was walking along one winter's day through an alley, when he saw someone he owed money to. He walked faster and then hid in a rubbish bin. The dealer found him hiding and he was with a load of butch men with checked jackets and anchor tattoos. They started to beat him up and poke him with sticks.

They left him in pain and his nose was bleeding. Joe started to drag himself to the street where other people poked and kicked him. He tripped up and fell flat on his face and there in front of him he saw a diamond watch. Joe had hit the jackpot!

He went to the nearest pawn shop and got billions of pounds for it. He went to America and bought the Playboy mansion.

Joe is now called Justin Timberlake!

Victoria Cowley (11)
Fairfield Primary School, Penarth

A DAY IN THE LIFE OF A SCUBA-DIVER

This morning I woke up at 7am. I got dressed and then went down to the café for my bacon sandwich. I put on my dry suit and rode down to Little Haven to launch the boat.

Once the boat had been launched, we all put on our masks, fins and cylinders, did our zips up and set off for Stack Rocks. When we got there, we put the boat into neutral and threw the anchor over the side of the boat. I partnered up with Adrian and left Theresa and Ted to look after the boat.

When we had finished the buddy check, I followed Adrian, doing a backwards roll off the side of the boat. I signalled to Adrian to go down and we slowly descended, seeing lots of marine life including conger eels, wrasse and one seal.

When we got to the bottom, a great white shark came at us and we went to the surface as fast as we could. We got into the boat as the shark came shooting out of the water with an octopus around its head wrestling it to the bottom of the ocean. Will the shark come back for me or not?

Ashley Jones (11)
Fairfield Primary School, Penarth

A DAY IN THE LIFE OF A POUND COIN

It was 6am and I was nice and snug in my black velvet purse. Suddenly, I heard the zip undo and then I heard a shouting noise:
'Emma, I'm just popping out for some milk. OK?'
'OK, mam.'

It was a bumpy ride in my small purse. Up and down and all around. Once we were there, I was dumped fiercely on the counter. I was taken from my home - my purse. I was placed carefully into the shop owner's sweaty hands. They were so sweaty that I could have melted, but I pulled myself together.

The next person I came across was an old and frail woman. She had the boniest hands you could ever imagine and those stupid hands almost scratched my shiny, smooth and golden coat.

Suddenly, I heard a sweet and innocent voice. I was guessing it was a new place for me, even though I'd only been here less than 10 minutes. Anyway, I was being slowly taken out of the till as the customer and shopkeeper were having a conversation.

Finally, I was placed in his hand. It was a small and very uncomfortable hand indeed as it was so sticky from the sweets. Guess what? I almost stuck to him and it was the most disgusting experience I have ever had.

But the last place I was going was the local community's leisure centre vending machine and well, that has been my home ever since, which has been a whole three months.

Laura Giles (11)
Fairfield Primary School, Penarth

THE MISSING TIGER

One day in a zoo in Africa, a tiger had escaped. It made its way to Cape Town and when it got there, it headed for the butcher's shop to eat. When it got thirsty, it made its way to the river to have a drink. It saw a group of people so the tiger chased them and then it caught a 35-year-old man and killed him. Then he got chased by the army into the rainforest.

When the tiger thought he had lost the army, they shot a tree right by its head. The tiger ran back towards the zoo when it got shot in the thigh. It struggled on and when it got back, the tiger was rushed to the animal hospital. After two months the tiger was fine.

Grant Beedell (11)
Fairfield Primary School, Penarth

A Day In The Life Of A Tesco Trolley

Whizzzz! Crash! Ouch! That hurt. Why does it always happen to me? These silly wheels need waxing! Here comes a customer. Hey up, freeze! She's got a dog and a few kids with her. Gosh! She must be stressed.
It looks like it's going to be a long day today.

Oh yes, I haven't introduced myself yet, have I? I am Wolly the whizzing trolley! Most of the other trolleys think I am mad because I run around like a headless chicken, but then I crash and get badly hurt. I'm being wheeled into the supermarket now. It's a bit boring being a trolley, but sometimes it can be great fun.
We're coming up to the milkshakes now. She's turning her back on me. I'm a bit dehydrated, so I think I might have maybe a weeny little sip of that frothy chocolate milkshake that's sitting by itself on that cold shelf. Yeah! That's the best thing that's happened to me all morning!
'Morning Jimmy, my friend.' He is my bestest pal. He is the only trolley that has never made fun of me in my trolley life.
There go the chimes for 12 o'clock. Lunchtime!
Ooo! Yum, yum! Look at all that greasy food sitting on that counter waiting to be eaten!

Right, we've had our lunch now, time for serious shopping! We are going along the aisles now. This lady has so much food and things in me now, I think I'm going to collapse. Around these long corridors we go, picking up bits and pieces from the white, glowing shelves.
It's getting dark outside now. The lady is paying at the till for her shopping. She wheels me back in between the shiny, reflecting metal bars where the trolleys are kept. Yawn! I am getting tired. I think I might . . . just . . . go . . . to . . . sleep . . . now. Yawn! Snore.

Sophie Roberts (10)
Fairfield Primary School, Penarth

THE OONGA WOONGA MASK

Odo stood there, sweat rolling down the side of his face. He was of the Tribe of the Three. He had dark brown skin, black hair and his brown eyes were so dark, they could have been black.

He was witnessing the execution of a trespasser. The man who was being led to the chief priest was pale-skinned. He had a wide-brimmed hat, a white, crumpled shirt, brown trousers and a black belt.

Odo was disgusted with his tribe's mutated form of justice and when he was old enough he would set off for the western world, but for now he would have to live with it. You see Odo was only 14 and he had planned to leave when he was 15. Unfortunately, one year seemed a long time.

His tribe possessed the Oonga Woonga mask - a treasured gift thought to have been given by the gods. Odo wandered off, not wanting to be involved in the gore of the events he knew would follow. He walked to the biggest hut, surrounded by guards, where the Oonga Woonga mask lived. He looked at the mask. It was a shining gold, which could probably blind you on a sunny day. It had bright neon-coloured feathers poking out of the top. He stared up at the mask and it stared back. He didn't know how long he looked at it, but he finally left.
He was standing outside when his father approached.
'Odo, I have some amazing news. The brethren of priests have decided to accept you. Isn't it great?'
Odo was speechless.

Odo would have to make his escape plan for tomorrow. He walked over to the cooking tent to get supplies for the journey.

That night he couldn't sleep and he kept turning over on the soft bracken. He woke at dawn, picked up his pack and left the peaceful-looking village.

Calum Brunt (11)
Fairfield Primary School, Penarth

A DAY IN THE LIFE OF A GHOST

Hi, my name is Michael and last night I had the maddest dream. I became a ghost and I was able to go through walls, doors and could even float in the air. It felt amazing. I felt really lively and energetic, so I went to do a little scaring.

First I went to my English teacher's house because she would always move me when I was having a laugh. I gave her an extra scare. I held pictures up and chucked lamps across the room. She could only see things flying around.

Later I decided to go to Gareth's house and there I also did a bit of scaring to wake him up. Finally he woke up and I told him that he had to hold on to the brush that I was giving him and he would stay invisible like me, so he should keep it in his pocket and come with me.

So off we went to the house I came from. We had such a laugh. We pulled chairs from under her, moved the clock forward and took some chocolates, like in Matilda.

Finally, after a few hours, we thought we would play our last trick. We conjured up man-eating iguanas. She jumped up and down on the furniture screaming at the top of her voice, even though no one could hear her. We decided to leave her in peace with the man-eating iguanas. Hopefully, no one ever saw her again.
Please let that be the case!

Michael (11)
Fairfield Primary School, Penarth

THE MAN IN THE MOON

He woke up at 7.30 this morning to find that someone or something had been eating his cheese. He was so angry. He didn't know who, or what it was. 'I think someone's here. I'm no longer alone. I will not rest until I find this fiend,' he cackled.

He walked back to his hut to grab a snack before he went to kick some serious butt! Mind you, Mak's snacks aren't really snacks, they're more like three-course meals. He had a chicken breast topped with bacon and melted cheese and smothered in BBQ sauce, dripped with extra moon cheese. He then left.

He searched all over the moon, but could find no one. All he could find were more holes appearing and more cheese disappearing. Mak started to get hot and dizzy. The moon was rotating and seemed to be getting closer to the sun, yet he had only just noticed. Mak thought for a minute, then quietly said to himself, *'My golly gosh, my moon is melting!'*

Yasmin Spear (11)
Fairfield Primary School, Penarth

A HOLIDAY IN HELL

The girls were still packing, although they started early in the morning. Almost everyone was packed, except for Chloe and Hannah. They were nowhere near finished. Kim, Rachel, Lisa, Chelsy and Katrina struggled to carry their luggage to the taxi which had been waiting for two hours. Chloe and Hannah finally finished and dragged their bags to the taxi.

'God,' huffed Hannah, 'you'd think the stupid, fat driver would help us!'

'Yeah, you'd think he would,' shouted Chloe to give the driver a hint.

They arrived at the airport and still the driver wouldn't help them.

'Ugh,' Chloe huffed and paid the driver half the price. She stomped into the airport. The driver tried to run after her, but he was out of breath in no time.

They got onto the plane and Chloe was still moaning. 'What a rude and ugly driver!'

'OK, we get the point,' the other girls shouted.

They arrived at daring Devil's Island and they were astonished. At the beginning of the flight the plane was white with a Virgin logo on the wing. Now it was bright red with flames on it. They were then dragged off by a devil. They were dragged into a red room surrounded by fire. A devil-looking creature came up through the flames and tied the girls up. The girls were wriggling and screaming as the devil tried to push them into the flames. Then Buffy the devil slayer barged in, stabbed the devil and untied the girls.

'Thank you so much,' they said.

Kim McCarthy (11)
Fairfield Primary School, Penarth

THE FACELESS GHOST

'This ghost has no face, you see,' he began. 'It wanders the Earth searching for a face. If it catches you, it takes your face and your body too. It gets you when you're sleeping - just lies down and takes over your body. The process takes six hours in all. If you wake up before the end, you're safe. If not, there you are, a ghost without a face. You look down and see your body, your face, but it's not you. The ghost has got it now and it takes over your life. You're the faceless ghost, searching for someone, someone you can take over, get their body, get their face, get their life,' whispered Sam.

'Oh my God. There's something behind me! I'm all itchy,' freaked Nakita.

They were in a tent. Just Sam, Nakita and Phil, camping in his garden.

'I know! Let's go down to the crippled shack where this all started off - the story I mean.'

'What, to see if it's true? To see if there is a faceless ghost there?'

'Yeah.'

They carefully unzipped the tent and set off with torches, hats, coats and plastic guns.

After twenty minutes they were at the tumble-down house and they cautiously crept inside to find blurred shapes floating around.

'Six, five, thirty-six. Six, five, thirty-six.' Nakita kept repeating these numbers.

'Let's get out of here!'

The next day, when they were in the tent, they saw that Nakita hadn't woken. Six, five, thirty-six. Today. She hadn't woken up yet because *she was dead!*

Jessica Mumby-Price (11)
Fairfield Primary School, Penarth

THE SUIT OF THE ODO

It was a horrid day when the Odo suit was found. It seemed like yesterday when the world was doomed.

It was a normal day for me looking around the ancient Egyptian pyramids and I came across a dead end. I started to feel to see if there were any trapdoors, but there weren't, there was a trap floor.

The floor moved and everyone fell down. We came out into a room with thousands and thousands of gold coins in it. The best thing was we had found the legendary Odo tomb and there he was, just lying there, no traps, no guards, nothing. So we all stared at him and I lifted off his suit to look at it and to take it to a lab to examine it more carefully. The others looked at the body. The suit was initially made out of gold and diamonds. It had a cobra snake on the top, plus the shape of a bear in the middle.

One day they were looking carefully at the Odo and suddenly it got up. Its eyes glowed like shining gold. It screeched out in a mighty voice, 'Where is my suit!'
Everybody ran as fast as they could out of the building. The Odo made the building crash to the ground and he almost made the whole world explode, but then I came and gave him the suit. Amazingly, he stopped and went back to the cave where he was found.

Andrew Taylor (11)
Fairfield Primary School, Penarth

THE SPECIAL EGG

In a barn on top of a hill some barn animals live. It was a very sunny morning and the barn animals were sound asleep. There was no sound coming from the barn, except one. It was Charlie chicken. Charlie was always awake at the crack of dawn every morning. Then finally Lucy goose woke up, then the chickens and cockerels. There was still one animal asleep - Hannah hen. She was asleep all morning.

It was finally the afternoon and Hannah was awake. She stood up and walked over to the animals. Their mouths dropped. Hannah had laid an egg, a very special egg. It wasn't the same as any other.

The next day Charlie was up first, as always. Then everyone else woke up, including Hannah. The only thing was that Hannah's egg was gone. Hannah didn't know what to do. That day every animal looked for the egg. In the afternoon Hannah sent everyone out to the farm. They all looked high and low, but no one went to Farrell fox's den. No one had the courage to. Then Charlie chicken said that he would go. He crept to the fox's den, very quietly, then he crept into the den. Luckily Farrell fox wasn't there.

He searched the den, but he couldn't find the egg. He looked again and there it was - Mrs Fox's special gold-plated box. Mrs Fox wouldn't allow anyone to open it. Charlie went over and opened the box carefully. Hannah's egg was painted gold and stood on a little red cushion. Charlie took it carefully and went back to the barn. Hannah was so happy.

Meanwhile, at Farrell fox's den, Mrs Fox was not happy

Hannah was trying to get the gold off the egg. When it wouldn't come off, she called it 'the special egg'.

Enith Jones (10)
Fairfield Primary School, Penarth

THE TWO MAGIC PENS

It was the last day of the summer holiday and Jemma was at 'Pens R Us'. Jemma goes every week to choose two pens she likes the best. This time she didn't choose any old two pens, she chose the two magic pens. She asked the shopkeeper how much a pen is.

The shopkeeper said, 'A pen costs £2.50, don't forget, it's a magic pen,' replied the shopkeeper politely.

Jemma ran to her mum as quickly as possible to ask if she was allowed these two pens. 'Am I allowed these two pens Mum?'

'How much do they cost?' replied Mum,

'Ummm, they cost £5,' answered Jemma,

'They're expensive, but yes.'

Next day she went to school and she had art class. Her teacher Mrs Gilbert asked them to draw one single picture. Jemma had her magic pens in school. She had a yellow and a blue. She took the lid off the yellow one.

'Put your sunglasses on,' sang the yellow pen.

Everybody was on the sun.

'It's really hot up here,' said the whole class. Jemma put the lid back on. Everybody was back in class.

'Wow! These pens are magic,' said Jemma amazed. She took the lid off the blue pen. Everybody was surfing. Jemma put the lid back on quickly. Everybody was back in class. Mrs Gilbert was very cross and the pens disappeared.

Joseph Keenan (8)
Fairfield Primary School, Penarth

THE SPOOKY HOUSE

Once upon a time there was an old house and one dark, cold night Bill had his friends over and he said, 'Why don't we go to the old scary house?'
They said, 'Yes let's go now, that's a great idea.'

When they got to the house, they opened the door and went in and the door shut behind them, they could hear a loud noise and got scared. Suddenly the lights went off and someone with a lamp said, 'Get out of this house or I will have to kill you.'
They said, 'It is an old house, you cannot make us go.'
Then the strange voice said, 'I will have to kill you.'

They started to fight. Bill, Nat and Tom killed the bad man and went back to Bill's house and told his mum all about the fight and they never went there again.

When a different house was left by its owners, Bill said, 'Let's go in that house.'
They all said, 'Can't you remember what Mum said about never going in the house again?'
Bill then remembered what his mum had said and the man that was there.

Natasha Williams (11)
Fairfield Primary School, Penarth

SPOOKY ISLAND

One day John, Adam and Bill were at the airport and they were all going to Spooky Island. They sat next to each other on the jumbo jet. When they got out of the plane at the airport, they saw a castle and Adam said, 'Let's check that castle out on the mountain.'
Bill and John said, 'OK.'

Bill pulled out his CD player and put the speakers in his ears and when they reached the castle, they knocked on the door and it creaked open and they walked in. It looked like a playground as it had all theme park stuff in there. There was roller coasters, swings and roundabouts. Then they heard a spooky noise. It sounded like a ghost haunting the castle. They walked into a panel room and saw a man through a panelled window. Adam walked out of the room and went to see if there was any fingerprints on the glass but there wasn't any glass.

All of a sudden, he saw a piece of glass under the panel and said to Bill, 'I have found a piece of glass.'
They then went to watch a baseball match and they caught the robber, it was Mr Jones, our pilot.

Liam Wingren
Fairfield Primary School, Penarth

PUPPY IN THE FROST

'Yawn,' Laura had woken up and it is snowing. 'Mum can I have breakfast now? Plus I need to feed the cats.'

'OK but don't scream or you will wake up your dad.'

Laura ran downstairs, fed her 7 kittens and 2 cats. When she had finished she got herself some orange juice and put toast in the toaster. She also took a tray of juice and toast upstairs. She gave toast and juice to her mum and took the other to her dad and then went downstairs to eat hers.

Ding-dong, ding-dong.

'Eeaah!' Laura opened the door and Lucy was there.

'Hi Laura, coming out?'

'I need to get changed. Come in and I'll go and get changed, you go and watch TV or play with the cats.' Laura got changed and they went out.

'Ugg I think I stood on something and it hurt.'

'Oh dear,' Lucy said. Laura cried and then Lucy said, 'What a good idea, let's dig.'

'OK I'll get spades,' Laura said.

Laura and Lucy dug and dug. 'I have found something,' they both said at the same time.

Lucy explained that she could hear something and in the end Lucy found 10 little Labradors and 2 other dogs. Lucy took them all home and made a home for them in a dog basket with a big pillow and a baby quilt.

Stephanie Petherick (10)
Fairfield Primary School, Penarth

A Birthday Dream

It was a dark night in Ella-May's bedroom.

'Zzzz, zzzz.'

Knock, knock, knock.

'Come in, oh hi Lucy, do you know if Kacey's coming?'

'Yeah she's here now.'

Lucy and Kacey walked upstairs to put their bags down.

'Now, what do you want to do?

'Let's talk about boys,' whispered Ella-May making sure her mum didn't hear.

'Oh did you see James at school today?' as they all whispered to each other.

'Yeah.'

'Didn't he look lush in his football shoes, top and shorts?' said Kacey telling them clearly.

'Of course, anyway he looks cute in anything he wears,' said Lucy with a grin on her face.

'Girls, do you want anything to eat?' said her mum in the background of all the whispering.

'Yes please Mum.'

'OK I'll bring it up in a minute.'

'Now let's talk about something else,' said Ella-May in a louder voice.

'What shall we talk about then?'

'Let's not talk, why don't we play the limbo?'

'Yeah!' shouted all of them one after the other.

Ella-May charged downstairs to get a pole and the sweets and food.

'Who's going first?'

'Me!' shouted Ella-May in a loud voice.

'OK me and Kacey will hold the pole.'

'Under I go.'

Bang! Kacey had dropped the pole and it had fallen on top of Ella-May.

'Argh!'

'What? What?' said Ella-May's mum.

'Mum I had a bad dream but I'm OK now.'

'OK.'

Samara Hawthorne (10)
Fairfield Primary School, Penarth

HARRY POTTER

'Harry Potter! When are we going on the coach to Hogwarts?'
'Tomorrow,' said Hermione.
'Can we go early on the 18th June? I want to see Ron Weasley, I haven't seen him for a year since my last birthday?'
'Are things going alright Harry?'

'Ron I am so glad to see you.'
'How did you get here?' said Ron to Harry.
'I got here by Hermoine's cat.'
They got to Hogwarts very early and the coach was coming.

Two months later . . .

Harry Potter, Ron Weasley, Hermione Granger are having a lesson on gardening with the teacher of gardening house with magic plants and the rest of the magic class. Harry and Ron were very upset because Hermione had fainted and went stiff.

Three weeks later Harry and Ron found a secret way to the Chamber of Secrets and they went down the tunnel and ended up in a tunnel of snakes, which they defeated.

Samuel Donovan (10)
Fairfield Primary School, Penarth

A STORMY NIGHT

One stormy night I was walking past a castle and I heard a noise. It was coming closer and closer. Me and my friends were scared so we ran to my house and hid under the blanket.

My mum said, 'What's going on here?'

We said, 'There is a noise in the castle.'

That night we went over to Leigh-Anne's house to sleep over for the night.

In the night we could hear the noises in the castle, there were people sleeping in the castle. Next morning, we all woke up and had breakfast. After breakfast we went back over to my house. At 11am my mum and dad were still asleep so I got the keys out of my pocket and opened my front door. My friends said, 'This house is a really nice house, it has a big back garden and a big front garden too.'

We took lovely photographs of the back and front gardens and went over to Jessica's house for dinner. When we had finished our dinner, we went upstairs to play with make-up. We dressed up as pop stars and I dressed up as Britney Spears. Jessica dressed up as Kylie and Leigh-Anne dressed up as Lisa Scott-Lee.

We then went back to the castle to see if there were any spooky noises but there weren't so we went in the castle. Inside there was a big picture of a princess who had lived there.

Zara Moreton (11)
Fairfield Primary School, Penarth

HENRY'S BAD DAY

One morning Henry woke up, Henry stretched his arms and legs and got up.

'Henry!' shouted his mother. 'Time for school.'

Henry was going to be late so he threw his clothes on himself and ran down the stairs. 'No time for breakfast, bye!' There was a big bang at the door.

Henry ran to school. When he got there, all of the children had gone in, he walked to the door.

The teacher said, 'Why are you late?'

'Um . . . um . . . ' mumbled Henry.

'Sit down,' said his teacher.

At play time Henry was asked to play football, Henry was on the best team. They started playing and five minutes into the game, Henry had the ball, he kicked it nice and high and there were windows in front of him. The ball hit the window and shattered the glass. 'Oh no,' said Henry. The teachers were very disappointed. Henry's bad luck was getting worse.

When Henry was going home, he went to the park. He didn't have any friends so he just sat on the swing and ate his half-eaten sandwich. When he got home his mum and dad heard about the window, they told him off and Henry was very upset and fell asleep. Now he would get out of the right side of his bed in future.

Rhys Owen (10)
Fairfield Primary School, Penarth

CAPTURED

One cold night I was heading home with my next door neighbour's Chloe and Hannah after a wicked party. We were nearly home when Chloe yelled, 'Help! Help!' and was sucked into the ground.

'Pull Hannah, pull!' I shouted but we were sucked in too!

'Help!' we were yelling.

We ended up inside, down hanging over molten lava and saw Kim and Rachel.

'What are you two doing here and why did you miss the party?' Chloe yelled.

'Why do you think?' shouted Rachel in a mood.

'Well we forgot to mention that we are both spies,' Kim remembered to say.

'So are we!' Hannah said.

'Well it better be easy rope to cut and we can use our parachutes to move to the platform.'

'Yeah! That's a great idea!' remarked Kim.

So we did just that, we were finding the exit and saw a lot of lights and the man who had hung us up was being arrested. We were safe and sound and went home.

Katrina Georgiou (10)
Fairfield Primary School, Penarth

GHOST STORY

One evening in the summer holidays, my father decided to go out late night fishing. As there was no school the next day, my brother and myself asked if we could go along with him. He said that it was OK. We put our fishing gear together and we drove to a big, deep, dark pool about half a mile up the road.

We set up our fishing gear and then we cast our rods into the pool. We had to remain quiet so as not to scare the fish away. There was a deadly silence apart from the light rustle of the wind blowing through the trees and the rushes. All of a sudden, we heard splashes that sounded like someone walking through water. Then we saw a strange light coming from the pool about one hundred yards upstream.

My father was rather annoyed about the disturbance so he told us to reel in our lines so he could find out what was going on. To our amazement, there was a man standing in the middle of the pool with a torch and a net for poaching salmon and sea trout.
My father got very angry and he shouted out, 'You cheat, I will report you to the bailiffs, what is your name?'
With this, the man turned and laughed and he calmly walked away with a fine sea trout in his hand.

We thought we would follow him to see where he would go and to get the number of his car for the bailiffs. He went through a hole in the hedge and we quickly went after him. As we got through the hole in the hedge, all we could see was a big, vast open space with nothing around for miles. Where had this man gone? It was a total mystery.

There was nothing to do but collect our gear and be on our way home. We were very disappointed not to have caught this man.

On our way home, we noticed a light near the road. It was a farmhouse. We decided to knock on the door to see if we could borrow a phone to phone the bailiffs. Mr Jones, the farmer asked, what the problem was so we explained our story to him.

When he heard what we had to say he laughed out loud. He said to my father, 'You have no need to phone the bailiffs or worry about any fish going missing. What you saw was old Jack the poacher. He has been dead for over sixty years now and all you saw was his ghost that comes back every now and then, the fish you saw him catch was the same one he caught sixty years ago.'

After our chat about Jack we all had a lovely cup of tea with him and we were on our way home but we will remember this night for evermore. The night we met Jack the poacher.

Melanie Thomas (11)
Llanybydder Primary School, Dyfed

A DAY IN THE LIFE OF A CALF

Hello, my name is Dave and I'm a short-horned, bull calf. I've been living in this old, grey, cold place that humans call sheds with yellow stuff on the floor, it's nice to eat. They feed me white stuff from the cows.

Yesterday I heard the humans talking about something and if I am not mistaken, they were talking about me and my friends being moved. I don't like this place anyway so I hope the new place will be better.

What's that noise? It's getting louder. I don't like it. Hey why is a human opening the gate? They're telling us to get out! Yes, we're free! Hey, what's this silver thing. It's a trailer. Help! Help! Argh! We're moving, help!
'Shut up Dave,' shouts John
'OK,' I reply.

We're flung from side to side like a swaying ship. Wow! This place is good, there's green stuff on the ground. I think it's the stuff my mum calls grass. I can run about and jump and it's nice to lie down on the soft grass. I'm going to love it here.

Aled Davies (11)
Llanybydder Primary School, Dyfed

A Day In The Life Of A Homeless Cat

Today I am very hungry because I haven't had any food for days. I've been scrounging through dustbins in dark alleyways since my owner kicked me out of my home. Soon I realised about the cold winter evenings, so I had to find a house to stay in or I would die of hunger or freeze to death.

I desperately searched for someone to take me in. Luckily I found a house which looked warm so I scratched at the door and begged. Hopefully they will take me in but that didn't happen so I curled up inside an old cardboard box to try and keep warm. I was very weak, I was so weak I couldn't move. Soon a ginger cat came past with a mouse in its mouth so I begged for some of it. Luckily he gave me some so I had enough energy to drag myself into an alleyway. I felt very tired by now so I went to sleep, I just managed to make it through the night.

In the afternoon a person threw out their garbage, so I rumaged through to find some food to eat. I found a half-eaten chicken so before another cat came along I quickly ate it. I ran up a tree to see if there were any baby birds in the nest to eat, there weren't any birds so I climbed down the tree. When I reached the ground I smelt a nice smell so I followed the trail, it led to a roast dinner. I jumped onto the window sill, there was a boy playing with a strange object. The boy saw me and picked me up and took me to a woman. He asked the woman if he could keep me, the woman looked nice so I jumped on her lap and she said 'yes'.

I lived happily ever after with my new owner and they called me Max.

Fabian Driver (11)
Llanybydder Primary School, Dyfed

A Day In The Life Of A Dog

I woke up this morning as fit as a fiddle after my good night's sleep. I had my breakfast and then I went for my morning walk with my owner.

We went to the woods for a walk and I went over to a tree. I saw a squirrel and began to chase it but it was too fast and it got away. I walked back to my owner and carried on with my walk.

After a while, we turned around and began our way home. When we got home, my owner made me a big bowl of food. I then went by the fire and fell asleep.

Jamie Owen (10)
Llanybydder Primary School, Dyfed

A Day In The Life Of A Victorian Maid

This morning I got up for work from my gloomy attic room at 6am. I've got to light all the fires in the twenty-five rooms in the house. It takes about an hour to light the fires and I've got to dust the fireplaces, which are absolutely pitch-black because they are open fires.

At eleven o'clock Lady Elizabeth and Sir Henry get up for their breakfast and they've got to go out today because they've got an important meeting with the mayor of the town straight after breakfast.

Today Miss Lucy has got friends over because it's her birthday and she wants everything pink, but it's not me that has to cook it, I will have to serve the food though.

At last it's time for dinner, I have been working quite hard today and I'm tired because of my late shift last night. I hope it's lasagne for dinner, the cook's lasagne is absolutely divine. Oh what a shame, it's not what I was hoping for. It's shepherd's pie, I ate my dinner as quickly as I could and went to work so that I wouldn't have to work late tonight.

My first job of the afternoon was to put all of the clothes in everyone's wardrobe and open their curtains because they hardly ever open their curtains, they let me do it.

Time goes so quickly when you work, doesn't it? I'm on my way back to my frightful and gloomy attic. I light my candle so that I can change into my rag of a nightdress. I blow my candle out and go to sleep.

Heledd Thomas (11)
Llanybydder Primary School, Dyfed

A Day In The Life Of A Cat

'Miaow, miaow.'

Oh hello my name is Cuddles the cat. I'm two years old, I'm hungry and I want my food, oh here comes my owner. 'Miaow,' mmmmm sardines in jelly with biscuits, mmmmm that was nice, I'm going to go out the hole in the door now.

I'm out, it's lovely and warm and . . . something's there, oh it's only a silly bird. Let's go next door to see Pushka. Oh Pushka is in the bush over there. 'Pushka come here, it's only me. Do you want to come to the river?'

'Yeah!'

'OK come on then let's get moving. Come on Pushka you can jump up on the fence, come on yeah you're up, let's go through the bush and we'll be there.'

There's the girl from the farm. Miaow. She's stroking me, let's go to the edge of the river. 'Argh - oh no, I'm in the river, I'm going to drown, miaow, miaow.'

The girl from the farm is coming to help, I'm out of the water, she's taking me to the farm, oh the lights have gone out, I can see my house. I can see the hole in the door, why is she banging on the door? There's my owner. I'm in my owner's hands, she's putting me in my nice warm basket, I'm never going near the river again.

Amie Wagner (11)
Llanybydder Primary School, Dyfed

THE HEAD

It was a lovely day and Matthew, Carwyn and Sam were going on a camping trip in the woods. They walked six miles and by that time, it wasn't a lovely day, it had started to rain and be stormy.

The boys started to get scared and they tried to pitch the tent but the ground was too wet.
'What are we going to do?' Carwyn shouted at the other two.
'Look over there, it's a house, let's go in,' Matthew shouted.
They opened the old, squeaky door and went in.
'This house is creepy,' Carwyn said, quite scared.

The two others weren't scared at all, they were more busy thinking about food, so they went into the kitchen,
'Oh nothing to eat and I'm starving,' Matthew said. When Matthew and Sam were in the kitchen, Carwyn went up the creaky stairs to see what was up there.

He opened the first door and it was a bathroom but this wasn't like the other rooms downstairs, this room was clean and there wasn't a spiderweb in sight.

Carwyn gazed at the sparkling room. He looked inside the bath and it was as clean as a whistle but when he lifted the toilet seat there was a big head staring at him.
'Argh!' Carwyn screamed as he was running down the stairs.
'What's wrong?' Matthew asked.
'There's a head in the toilet,' Carwyn said nervously.
'Don't be silly!' Sam said.
'Oh yeah there is, go up and have a look.'

Matthew and Sam went up to the bathroom and there it was again, the boys were shocked and they ran down the stairs and never came back again.

Emma Jones (11)
Llanybydder Primary School, Dyfed

A Day In The Life Of Julius Caesar

I'm in a good mood today. This morning I fed five whole slaves to the lions and two to the crocodiles and of course I got twice as much money for taxes today than yesterday. The people of Rome just love me ever since I conquered Britain. Yes now all their roads are straight.

Ah, look, it's my chief senator. 'What's the matter Cornilius?'
'Some people think you're trying to be king and they don't like it.'

Ah now that's sorted I can go and have my supper, I told Cornilius to give the idiots who don't like me a feast in their honour, people might want revenge if I fed them to the lions.
I'm going to the feast now. As a matter of fact it was going to be my supper but if I have to share I will.

'Ah hello people,' I say.
'Good day Caesar,' says a grumpy-looking man.
'Quiet now, dig in,' I reply.
'No way, it's probably poisoned.'
How dare he say that. I am giving him five pounds of chicken, ten apples, a salad with tomatoes and the biggest slice of bread Rome has ever seen and all he can say was it's probably poisoned. I should feed him to the lions right now. No he'll be expecting that. I'll just say to forget about the poison as I don't want anybody else to know either.

I walk away. That will show the grumpy and ugly man. I know, I'll go and have a private supper, yes with Mr Fluffy and Timmy teddy and Carl the croc.
Ahhh I . . . do . . . believe . . . I've . . . . been . . . stabbed . . . in . . . the . . . back. Goodnight.

Peter Davies (11)
Llanybydder Primary School, Dyfed

A Day In The Life Of A Cat

Today I got up at nine o'clock and saw that my owner wasn't there. I went downstairs and saw a massive bowl of cat food but I won't eat it unless I have to. I decided that I was going to hunt for mice instead.

When I came back I saw a dog in my house. I couldn't believe it, how cheeky! I asked her what her name was.
'My name is Lucy,' she said.
'My name is Tiddles,' I told her.
My owner appeared and gave the dog a big bowl of food. I didn't like this, the dog then started eating my food as I leapt forward to eat it. My owner put the food outside for me so Lucy couldn't get it.

Lucy was trying to get my food but she couldn't get over the gate. In the end, she jumped up and hurt herself, my owner wasn't about and I was the only one to help Lucy.

I went over to my owner for some help. I miaowed for a bit but she didn't understand. I then went to see Lucy and she was whining painfully in her basket. I climbed up on the table and knocked a mug down. That made my owner come in and she saw Lucy. My owner took Lucy to the vet.

Me and Lucy are now best friends!

Angharad Evans (10)
Llanybydder Primary School, Dyfed

A Day In The Life Of Busted

Today I am going in my limousine to sing live in Cardiff. Me and my mates are very excited because this is the first time we are performing live. We will be singing in front of 10,000 people so wish me luck. We will be singing our new hit single which is called 'Crush'.

I am in my limo right now and I am just having a bit of water because I am sweating. In my limo, there are my guitarists and some of my drummers. I am very nervous because if I make a mistake or do some Busted moves wrong, I might fall. Tonight when I am performing, I am going to wear my trainers, my shorts and my T-shirt.

We now have arrived at Cardiff Arena and me, James and Charlie are shaking like earthquakes. We are parked outside the Arena and I am going backstage in five minutes and I am performing in ten minutes but before we perform, me and the boys have to go and do our hair, ready to spike it up while the band set their stuff up.

Now we are ready to perform and the crowd out there are wild and noisy. Wish me luck because we're going out there.

'Hello everybody.'
'Hello.'
'We are going to sing our new hit single, 'Crush.'

That was great, now I am going to change and go in my sauna because I am hot, well, thank you for wishing me luck. Bye.

Meinir Williams (11)
Llanybydder Primary School, Dyfed

A Day In The Life Of Rachel Stevens

Today I'm going for a photo shoot in London, then later I'm in the studio recording my new album called 'Right Here'.

I'm in my Limousine right now on my way to London, I'll be there in about 20 minutes. I'm wearing my brand new top and skirt which I bought yesterday while shopping in Cardiff. You've got to look your best these days, the press are everywhere.

I've arrived just on time, now let's go in. Wow! This place is massive, not to mention posh.

Hey look there's Victoria Beckham. There's someone walking towards me.
'Hi! Are you Rachel Stevens?'
'Yes I am.'
'Can you follow me please?'

Look at all these clothes, better put them on. I've never had a photo shoot before, and an hour went quickly.

I'm now on my way to the studio. I think I'll have some wine and watch TV until we arrive there.

We're now in the studio, I'm practising my vocals right now. This is my first album since going solo.

The first song I'm singing is 'Don't Stop' which has been number one. My other single that has been released is called 'Right Here'.

Well, that was now over with, it was really nerve-racking and exciting. I hope loads of people will buy it.

It's got fourteen songs on it and a duet I did with Robbie Williams, which is cool.

I'm on my way home now to go to bed because I've had such a tiring day.

Wendy Davies (11)
Llanybydder Primary School, Dyfed

GHOST STORY - THE HOUSE

One night, Louise was playing in the park with her friends. It was half-past five and it was dark already, so they decided to tell scary stories.
'Then the ghost went, and the monster ate her,' Sarah said.
'Argh' they all screamed, then suddenly they all heard a noise. It was Louise's mobile phone.
'Come home, it's supper time,' Louise's mum said.

She went home to her mum, dad, grandma and grandad. When she arrived home, her grandad decided that they would go for a walk the next day, just Grandad and Louise. The next day Louise and her grandad went for the walk.

They stopped to play in the park for a while and then stopped to watch the football match in the field and as they walked on, they came to a big black house with no lights.
'Grandad, who lives in that house?' Louise asked.
'Well dear, that house has stood for a whole two hundred years. You see, in that house there lives spiders and no one knows what else,' Grandad replied.
'No one knows at all,' Louise said,
'Well there was this one man before, he went into that house without thinking and he walked into the kitchen and opened the cupboard and out flew a ghost so he ran to the door to get out but it was locked. He didn't know how to get out so he grabbed a baseball bat and tried to hit the ghost but it just went through it and no one has heard of him since,' Grandad said.

'Wow, that's a good story you made up Grandad,' Louise said as she was laughing.
'Oh I didn't make it up, it's true.'
Louise didn't believe her grandad so she thought that she would see for herself. She went to get Sarah and in they went.
The floors creaked, she opened the kitchen door and, 'Argh!' they screamed. There was a ghost so they ran into the front room and there was another one, so they ran upstairs and opened a closet.

Inside the closet was a skeleton, they ran back downstairs and they opened the door and ran home.

'Grandad,' Louise said.
'Yes?' he replied.
'That house you told me about, I believe you now.'
'Did you go in the house?' Grandad asked.
'Yes and the front door was open for us to get out.'
'Really, wow that's a mystery,' Grandad said, clueless.

No one ever went into the house ever again after they had heard the ghost story.

Kelly Jacob (11)
Llanybydder Primary School, Dyfed

A DAY IN THE LIFE OF A CAT IN A NEW HOME

When I woke up this morning I wasn't in my basket with my brothers and sisters, I was on, I think, what people call a bed. I've seen something like this before in the old farmer's wife's house. Anyway I decided to walk up the bed. When I had reached the top I saw a little girl which I'm sure I've seen before in the old farmer's house.

After looking at this girl thinking that she would wake, I decided to lick her in the face. Suddenly she woke up, she picked me up and put me in her lap and stroked me gently. Her stroking made my spine tingle.

Then after stroking me, she took me downstairs and put me in a basket. I watched her walk away from the basket to her mother. I do wish I was with my mother and father and brothers and sisters now. I turned around - my sad smile turned into a happy smile. I saw my mother and father and my brothers and sisters, I smiled with joy. Then the little girl's mother gave us four bowls of milk. Then I suddenly remembered that I was staying here with my family because we were too much for the farmer's wife and she couldn't look after us because she was too old.

Daniella Beaumont (9)
Llanybydder Primary School, Dyfed

A NIGHT AT MY AUNTIE'S HOUSE

One day I went to visit my Auntie Tina and she asked me if I'd like to sleep over her house that night, well I said yes and went home to pack my bag.

On the way home, I heard a bang on the front of the car, so I stopped and looked what it was. When I got out of the car to have a look, there was nothing there so I went back to the car and drove off home.

When I got home the phone rang. I answered it and there was no one there. This was starting to scare me.

I went to my room to pack my bag and I went outside but my car wasn't there. I went to phone Tina but my phone was dead. I went back outside and my car was there where I left it, so I got in to it and drove off to Tina's house.

When I arrived I went upstairs to unpack my bag and I went to the living room where my cousin Nigel was watching TV. Then suddenly the electric went off. Then we heard someone shout my name. 'Yes,' I said. Suddenly something touched me. I looked to see what it was. It was Malcolm.

I went up to the room I was sleeping in and went to sleep. Next morning I woke up with someone calling my name so I went downstairs to see who was shouting my name, but nobody was there so I went to make some breakfast and went home.

Siona Evans (10)
Llanybydder Primary School, Dyfed

THE HAUNTED HOUSE

One Hallowe'en night, Kathy and Kate were really excited because they were going to have a Hallowe'en party. Their mum said to them that they could all go trick or treating.

That evening they ran home from school to help their mum get the food ready and lay the table. After they had done that, it was half-past four and it was going to take them an hour to get ready. While they were getting ready their mum mixed the water, flower and eggs together.

They had just finished getting ready when all the children started to come. They were all wearing costumes. 'Do you want to go trick or treating?' asked Mum.
'Yes please,' they all said.

Off they all went. They went round a lot of houses but they came across a house with an overgrown garden and a heavy arch door. They knocked on the door and the door opened with a large squeaking noise. When they were all in, the door slammed shut.
'Hello,' shouted Kate. As Kate shouted they could hear an odd noise. They all ran home.

After they got home they had some food and told their mum about it. They never went back to that house again.

Charlotte Murray (11)
Llanybydder Primary School, Dyfed

A DAY IN THE LIFE OF A HORSE

I woke up to the sound of the other running horses. They were running around really fast, so I joined in just for a little while so I could wake up. It was fun. After that I had a drink from the stream and ate some grass.

I went down to the gate and my owner came to get me, but I did not want to go because I did not want to leave my friends. I had no choice, I had to go, so I did.

Then my owner Sam brushed my mane. It was really long and black. After that she brushed my tail and my back. She is the best owner I ever had. Then after she gave me a brush she tacked me up and she rode me to the bridleway and back along the canal.

Then she put me in an extra field. She was making me canter. After that we went back to the farm. She untacked me and took my bucket, so I knew I was having my dinner. I have pony cubes and chaff with sugar beet.

She put some water in and gave it to me. I ate it all up and I had to go to poo, so I did. Then she mucked out my stable and took me to the field and she closed the gate and went to the stable.

Then she said goodbye. I went *neigh* and went back to my friends .We all went *neigh.* Then my owner came back to see me. That's what I thought anyway but she gave us all some hay.

After that she gave me a kiss and said goodbye again. I went *neigh* and my friends and I ate all of the hay. Then we all went running up the field, laid down and ate some grass and my friends and I fell asleep. We were altogether and my owner went home and had her dinner.

Megan Tilley (9)
Monnow Junior School, Newport

A DAY IN THE LIFE OF RIO FERDINAND

Eight o'clock I woke up ready for training. My alarm clock woke me up, ready.

I drove down to Old Trafford for training. All my mates were there, getting their training tops off the manager. They were doing dribbling first. Then we had a match. I scored from a header. Beckham crossed it and I headed it. Then it was half-time. I had a drink then I went back on.

After the match I signed autographs. When Beckham crossed it I shouted Rio. I had a drink of squash. In the end we won 3-1. It was a good match. We had celebrations because we won. It was good.

Then we all went home to my house and played football in my back garden because I've got a football net for my training so I can improve. I brought my teammates over for a game. It was brilliant. Sometimes we go down to the football stadium. We get all the boys down, then we go out. We do training nearly every day.

Luke Williams
Monnow Junior School, Newport

A Day In The Life Of A Fox

I woke up on Tuesday morning and I couldn't believe I was a fox. I went out hunting rabbits and birds but I couldn't catch them. They were too fast. I went chasing chickens. I sneaked in the chicken shed. I chased them out and ate the eggs. Then I ate a few chickens.

The farmer fired his gun. I didn't know where to go. The farmer was chasing me but I was too good for him. Then he fell over because he was too fast. That's why I got away. I called him Thunder but because his butt was too fat he tried to catch me with it.

In the end I got out of the farmer's yard. I carried a chicken in my mouth. I went down a big empty burrow to eat the chicken, then I hid because a rabbit came down. Then I went home with a full tummy.

Luke Roberts (9)
Monnow Junior School, Newport

A Day The Life Of Sabrina The Teenage Witch

Aunt Zelda woke me up by practising her singing for Mr Craft. I went downstairs and said, 'Can you be quiet please.'
Then silence for 20 minutes.
'Why should I be quiet?' said Zelda.
'Because it's distracting,' I said.
I got dressed, I had breakfast, toast and butter.

I went to school with Harvey and Hilary. We got to school. We did our test. I had A+, Hilary had B. Harvey had A+ too. We had lunch, gravy and mashed potato. Then we had science and then we went home. It was 4.00.

Me and my friends went out till 10.00 before going home. I went to bed.

Jamie Harris
Monnow Junior School, Newport

A Day In The Life Of Elvis

I was woken up by my alarm early in the morning to go to the stadium for the big day.

I got dressed and got my guitar ready. We got on the bus and we drove away to the stadium. I was pleased when I got there. There was a massive queue. When I got there there were already people in some of the seats. In twenty minutes I was going to sing on the big stage.

I sang for practise, 'We can't go on together with suspicious minds, suspicious minds.' I stopped then I went on stage to sing. When I finished we drove home and I went to sleep.

Jeremiah Shea (9)
Monnow Junior School, Newport

A DAY IN THE LIFE OF A RABBIT

I was woken up by the sound of birds singing and tweeting to the other birds. It was very bright and sunny. I went out to look for some grass because I was hungry. I heard a noise. It sounded like a fox.

I looked around and I saw a big, tall, brown thing. It went *woof, woof.* It was a dog. I turned around and ran as fast as I could and dived into my burrow. It was as scary as getting eaten by a bear.

My heart was beating like a drum. I was still scared. I peeped out of the burrow and the dog was gone. My friend came around to see if I wanted to go hunting. I said yes but I was still scared. She asked me why I was scared, I told her the whole story.

We met our neighbour. She came too. We hopped along. My friend saw some food. We all ate it and went home to sleep.

Brogan Keepin Davies (9)
Monnow Junior School, Newport

A Day In The Life Of Christina Aguilera

In the morning I was still asleep. My boyfriend woke me up. I got up and went to get dressed but I kept on singing. I got my clothes on and I went downstairs. I sang and my boyfriend said, 'Stop singing.' I said, 'OK.' Then I went in the living room and kept on singing. I went upstairs, went in the shower and washed my hair. I got out of the shower and I got ready.

I went to see my mother and when I went out I could not believe it. Oyer and my boyfriend came with me. His name is Justin Timberlake. He is fab. You've got to see him. My fab boyfriend and I were so surprised. We walked onto the mat outside. We were on a *love balloon*. I love him.

We had a little kiss on the *love balloon*. It was lovely as well. Then we went back home and went to bed. It was a long day and we had a long, long sleep. My boyfriend and I were very, very tired.

Danielle Miller
Monnow Junior School, Newport

A DAY IN THE LIFE OF MYSELF

One day at 9 o'clock I was running to school and I fell over. I looked to see what I'd fallen over. Then I found a two pound coin. I ran and ran to school. When I got there I ran into the classroom and I opened the door and stepped in and shouted, 'Sorry I'm late.' I gave in my dinner money for Wednesday and all the class was looking at me. I was so embarrassed.

I ran to my seat and cried. The children all laughed at me and laughed again and laughed and laughed because I was 15 minutes late and the class was halfway through science, my favourite subject. Then my teacher asked me why I was late. I said it was because I fell over and I lost my shoe. I got it back and I ran and ran to school and it was there.

It was nearly play time and then dinner time. After dinner we did some maths, had play, then art. Then I had to go home. We finished at 3.15. I played a game called Jenga. I won. We had our tea and I had a bath with my sister and my mum got her out. I was swimming in he bath. I fell asleep and my dad got me out and put me to bed.

Jodie Witch
Monnow Junior School, Newport

A Day In The Life Of Rhys

One very sunny day in the year 3000 it was Jake's birthday party. Jake had his party at The Supreme Sufleam Disco. They were having the time of their lives.

You would not guess what happened. A dragon (fire-breathing dragon) cut off the roof and threw it. It put its arms in to try and get some food. Luckily the dragon missed and accidentally took a chunk of the floor. Everyone started laughing at him. The dragon put his mouth in, Rhys threw drinks into the dragon's mouth. It tried to breathe fire, but it couldn't. It ran and ran until he was very far from them.
Everyone shouted, 'Hip hip hooray.'
It was rewarding. Rhys had his picture in the news and everything. Everyone in the world who heard about it was always nice to him, people gave him money and gold.

Now it was Rhys and Jake's party. It was the time of their lives and they'll never forget that amazing day, never, never and never . . . until the year 4000 when the trees and the flowers will always stay alive and there are robots all over the place.

Rhys Davies (9)
Monnow Junior School, Newport

A Day In The Life Of The Cheeky Girls

One day I was watching TV in my bedroom and it was about the Cheeky Girls. The people on the TV said you could meet them if you answered this simple question, who sings 'Take Your Shoesies Off'? and I rang up and said, 'The Cheeky Girls.'
Then a lady said, 'You can go to their concert tomorrow.'

Then I went to bed and in the morning I was very excited. The time came. I went to their concert and they sang, 'Take Your Shoesies Off' and 'Touch My Bum'. Everyone was cheering and then they came to get me and took me backstage and we went for a ride in a sports car to a restaurant.

We had a lovely dinner at the Royal Oak, then we went back to the concert and I sang with them. We had a lovely day, then we went to the hairdresser's and I had my hair like them. Then I went home with them.

Chloe Sully (9)
Monnow Junior School, Newport

THE BLOODSUCKING VAMPIRE

Saturday 27th of March 1997 at 7.00 in Japan I went to watch some TV to watch 'Goosebumps' and then I heard a roar. I said it must be the TV, then I heard it again. I was very scared. I sprinted upstairs and saw a vampire sucking the blood of my mother. My father punched the vampire and he turned into a bat and he spread snakes around the house. Inside he hid up in the attic. We covered Mum up and dug a grave in the garden.

Later I heard the noise again. The vampire was back. We ran as fast as we could, but a bomb blew up the garage and then we ran to the underground bunker. Then the vampire put a line of fire in front of us. My father said, 'I am going to throw you over the fire then go to the underground.'
I said, 'OK,' so he threw me over and ran to the underground. There were bombs dropping everywhere. I heard a sniper shot. I thought about my father. I saw the vampire. I saw a cross and held it up and he died.

Alex Parkhouse (8)
Penclawdd Primary School, Swansea

THE HAUNTED HOUSE

Once in Zombie Island there was a haunted house and there were four boys, their names are Sam, Ryan, Chrissy and Daniel. They went into the haunted house and they heard footsteps behind them. Then they heard, *'Whooo! Whooo! Whooo!'* They were freaked out. Then they heard it again. *'Whooo! Whooo!'*

It was 12.00 and the wolves started barking. Then they went upstairs and went into the attic and they found an old banjo and hit him over the head and he ran off. The boys ran downstairs and a ghost appeared, and they ran off home.

Samuel Devonald (9)
Penclawdd Primary School, Swansea

HAUNTED GHOST

One night at 12am there was a ghost in the bedroom. I was asleep. I saw a shadow on the wall. It looked like a ghost. It went downstairs. I followed it downstairs. The ghost saw me. I ran up to my bedroom, then I jumped out of the window. I hurt myself but I kept running for help.

Then the person next door came out and he was right behind him, but he ran with me then lost the ghost. We kept on running. The ghost took a short cut. We heard a *'Whoooo!'* And there was a dog barking all night.

The ghost caught us and killed the man but I got away. The ghost caught up and I killed the ghost. I went home. My mother, father and my sister were dead, so I called my friend in London and asked if I could stay with his family and friends. Then I lived with him and went to bed.

Daniel Nurse (9)
Penclawdd Primary School, Swansea

THE HAUNTED STORY

I woke up on Monday morning and it was Hallowe'en, then I got ready to go trick or treating. I painted my face then put my suit on. I walked out of the house and jumped in the car to go trick or treating.

First I went to my auntie and uncle's house, knocked on the door. It opened, but no one was there to trick or treat. I stepped into the house then the floor screeched! There floated a ghost. It was white and see-through. I ran out of the house and jumped into the car and went to nan's. My mum stopped the car at the driveway. I knocked on the door, my mum was still in the car on her mobile phone. My nan opened the door, my nan gave me some sweets. I went into the house, then I said thank you to my nan for the sweets. They tasted funny.

I jumped back into the car. I had a rest in the car but I couldn't rest. It was the sweet! What was it called? I picked up the wrapper. It was called a chewy sweet. I don't like chewy sweets. There's sherbet inside it. I jumped back into the car, back to my house. It was on fire with vampires in it. I screamed!

Daniel Keefe (8)
Penclawdd Primary School, Swansea

SLEEPOVER SCARY STORY

One day there was a little short house that belonged to Mr and Mrs Rees and their daughter, Samantha, my best friend in the entire world. Samantha had two sisters, one brother and one stepbrother. Samantha was the youngest. We either called her Sam, Sammy or Loops for short. She lives in Pendawdd and I live in Crofty. Sam is in the same school but she won't be any longer because I'm moving to Llanmorlous School which is closer to where I live. I will miss Sam because she has been my best friend since nursery. Even if I do move to Llanmorlous and even if I do meet new friends she will still be my best friend.

Well, that's all about me now because I am going to tell you about a scary time when I was sleeping over Sam's house. On Friday 21st December 2002 I slept over at Sammy's house and when we went into the house I saw a shadow, but there was no need to worry because it was Sammy's brother, Andrew. We call him Bug. So me and Sam went upstairs until I saw that shadow again but it was only Mindy, Sam's older sister. Then Sam's mum said, 'Girls, time for tea.'

'OK,' said Sammy, so we went downstairs and I saw that shadow again but it was only Rachel, Sammy's other sister. We ate our food then we watched 'Jeepers Creepers' which is a horror movie. I've watched it about four times and Sammy's only seen it once. So after we watched 'Jeepers Creepers' I went to bed and I saw that shadow again, but I thought it can't be any part of Sammy's family because they are all downstairs. *Who is it?* I thought. I screamed.

Next morning Sammy asked me, 'Do you want to sleep over again tonight?'
I said, 'No thanks! I think you better sleep over mine.'

Stephanie Bennett (9)
Penclawdd Primary School, Swansea

THE HAUNTED CASTLE

The characters in my ghost story are David, Mike, Dracula and the ghost.

One night there were two boys called David and Mike. They wanted to go to the shop for some sweets. They went to the shop to buy sweets. When they were on their way home they saw a castle. They decided to go inside. Inside there were cobwebs and skeletons. David and Mike got locked in a room and a cupboard opened. A ghost went whizzing out of the cupboard. He said, 'Your goal is to get a key to the front door and escape from the castle.' The ghost gave them a sword and shield. They thought that they would go in the TV room. There was a big bang in the TV room.

'It's the zombie guarding a chest,' said David. They fought against the zombie and killed him and that opened the chest. In it was a letter saying the key was right on the top floor.

They ran up 10 floors and there was a big monster with sharp teeth. They fought. David got hit and got knocked out. It was up to Mike to save the city. He threw his sword and hit the monster's brain and he got the key and escaped.

Corey Gunnell (9)
Penclawdd Primary School, Swansea

THE HUMAN SNAKE MAN

Saturday, 21st March 1987 at midnight in Southampton. I was in bed sleeping but I could not sleep. I heard a funny noise downstairs. I thought it was Mum and Dad but it was not Mum and Dad. It was someone else. I found somewhere to hide. It was a person with snakes all over him. I was lucky. It just looked in my bedroom and went. I said, 'Phew,' and I went to bed.

Next day I woke up and I was getting ready for school. When I got home I watched TV and did my homework. It was maths and when I finished I went back upstairs and played with my toys. He opened the chest to put the toys away and the man was in there with the snakes all over him. He gripped hold of me and dragged me to his hideout. He hung me up on the wall. I found a way out of there. I kept on kicking the wood until it snapped and when it snapped I made a run for it to my bedroom. He followed me but the police saw him, but he killed them. He saw me in the bedroom. He climbed the side of my house. There was a ladder. I went to phone the police.

The police surrounded the house and arrested him forever and ever.

Ryan James (9)
Penclawdd Primary School, Swansea

THE HORROR STORY

Now the day just started on a Sunday morning and it was Hallowe'en and I was going to dress up as a vampire. My name is Charlie. My other friends were dressing up as vampires too. One of my friends was coming with me. His name is John. We were dressed and just leaving the house.

We left the house and we walked down the street. A ghost was walking behind us and we looked at him and he looked at us and started running after us, so we ran as fast as our little legs could go. We ran behind houses and he found us. We went everywhere but he found us everywhere. He found us everywhere we were. He found us so we just ran straight and we looked behind us and there was a whole gang, so we ran even faster. We ended up in a dark tunnel and there was a trap. We fell down the trap into a pit. The ghosts fell down too. We found a way to get out and we got away safely.

We've lived fine since that day. Our mothers were shouting at us because it was way past our bedtime. Our fathers had fallen asleep so they could not shout at us.

Nathan McCarthy (9)
Penclawdd Primary School, Swansea

THE GHOST AND THE HOOVER

It all started in my friend Stephanie's house. It was scary, horrifying and beastly. I saw it and I shouted, 'It's a ghost!' I was running and running until I reached my house. When I got there I told my mother that there was a ghost in Stephanie's house and that I never want to go for tea and sleep over again.

I went back to see if Stephanie and her mum, Philippa, were alright. Thank the Lord they were alright. I was trying to be brave by sleeping over at Stephanie's, but I couldn't sleep.
That night I woke up and said, 'I am scared. Can we wake your mum up?'
'Yes,' said Stephanie.

The night after last I slept up there again and her dad got rid of the ghost by hoovering it up. I enjoyed sleeping over her house after that.

Samantha Rees (9)
Penclawdd Primary School, Swansea

A DAY IN THE LIFE OF BERGKAMP

This is the match of Arsenal vs Southampton in the FA Cup. The score was 1-0 to Arsenal and I will now tell you how that happened.

They all came running out of the tunnel and the game began. Then suddenly number 7, Pires, scored the winning goal. Then about five minutes later number 10 Bergkamp, who is 36, nearly scored the second goal. Then the whistle blew for half-time. The game began. Southampton nearly scored but Ashley Cole saved it with his leg and it went out for a corner. Then the whistle blew and the crowd went mad whistling and clapping. Then Arsene Wenger gave bottles of wine to shake and squirt all over the football pitch. Then all of the subs came on and started jumping to their song in joy.

After the match I was gutted that Bergkamp did not score and I thought that he should have been man of the match instead of Seaman. When Henry was talking Wiltord jumped onto Henry. Wiltord said, 'We have done it again.'
Henry said, 'We have not won the Premiership but we are happy we have won the FA Cup.'

Jessica Ronan (9)
Penclawdd Primary School, Swansea

THE FAKE GHOST

One evening Emma Clark was over her friend Amy Davies' house for a slumber party. Only Emma came because Amy was ginger. She was bullied because of it.

The next day they went to see the haunted house because a ghost had been coming around stealing things. Finally they arrived at the door.
'Are you still up for this?' said Amy.
'Yes,' said Emma.
Amy knocked. The door opened but no one was there. They went in and found a trail of green slime. It smelled like of pigs. They followed the trail to the ghost.
It said, 'Beware and get out of here!'

All of a sudden the ghost went all fuzzy, you know like a TV does and then it disappeared. They then heard a cough. They then found a robber hiding. The ghost was never real. He was just a reflection. The girls took him to the police.

Later they gave everyone their things back. Two days later they were in school, Amy was no longer bullied. Both girls were the most popular in school.

Katie Wallace (8)
Penclawdd Primary School, Swansea

A Day In The Life Of Mark Jones

It was the 10th of May and Llanelli were playing Newport. It was a hot, sunny and bright day. The roof was open. There was a big crowd. Mark Jones was playing. Lee Davis was captain. Newport were winning and then Mark Jones came trudging through and scored an unforgettable try. Everyone was cheering for Mark Jones.

Then it was half-time. The match continued. It was a superb game, but no one had scored. Mark Jones was playing on the wing at number 14. The supporters must have brought him very, very good luck because he went and scored an astonishing try. Everyone was shouting for number 14. Everyone was shouting for him. At the very end in about the last five minutes Finay scored an excellent try which made the final score 32-13. They had won the Principality Cup. They all lifted it and kissed it. They were all cheering and laughing.

Now Mark Jones and all the rugby players are going on tour to New Zealand with all the other rugby teams.

Rachel Tucker (9)
Penclawdd Primary School, Swansea

A DAY IN THE LIFE OF A FOOTBALL FAN

When I woke up in the morning I was in a football stadium. I can't remember my father booking tickets. Well I better enjoy the match, England coming up to score, David Beckham shoots and David Seaman saves the goal. The Arsenal fans are like a crowd of lions, so then Pires runs down the pitch and scores. The ref goes up to the commentator and the commentator yells down the microphone, *'Goal!'*

The fans scream, *'Goal!* Arsenal you can beat England!' The ref blows his whistle. The game ends. It is a disappointment to England, so they go to the tunnel and when Arsenal go in the tunnel they shake hands with England.

I say to the man sitting by me, 'Arsenal are good sports and a good team.'

Josh Eynon (9)
Penclawdd Primary School, Swansea

BECKHAM'S LAST HOUR

On Saturday 19th April 2003 David Beckham and his wife Victoria were just going to bed when David heard a noise, the kind of noise you hear when you've missed an open goal, so he went downstairs to see what it was. Then he heard a big *bang!* It was the bookcase falling down. Then from behind it he saw a werewolf. He screamed louder than Victoria would have.

Then he heard footsteps coming down the stairs, one after the other. David was petrified. Then he saw Victoria. She was wearing a pair of ear plugs.
'What's going on?' asked Victoria.
'It's a werewolf!' replied Becks.
Victoria couldn't believe it, but before she could say anything David was out of the door. Victoria with one kick knocked him out. She went to get Becks but he was dead on the doorstep. There was a cannonball painted like a football. There he was 53 yards away, Thierry Henry. He was wearing his football boots. Well it was pretty obvious that the cannonball had hit Beckham after Henry had kicked it. She fainted.

Jack Mountfield (9)
Penclawdd Primary School, Swansea

SCARY LIBRARY

It all started when I went to the library. Oh, I forgot to tell you, my name is Jimmy and my sister's name is Lily. I know, it's a funny name. My friends' names are Mickey, Paul, Peter and Daniel. Lily's friends are called Milly, Molly, Holly, Jessica and Rachel. Lily is a bit of a weird girl. She brings Rachel as a spare friend.

We found that the library was open till midnight. We asked our mum if we could go and she said yes.
'Can I buy a book too Mum?'
'Yes, OK.'

So we went and I could not believe my eyes. It was dark and the lights didn't work, so we looked around to see if we could find any candles. We tried to see if we could find Shauna, who works behind the counter, but we couldn't find her anywhere.

We heard funny noises. I thought it was very scary. Lily and me and my friends all split up and we all got lost in the library. In the end it was a tape, so I took it home, but the next night they heard the noise again.

Samantha Leanne Nurse (9)
Penclawdd Primary School, Swansea

THE GHOST AND THE LOST DOG

Faraway in a wood was a cottage with a very long and narrow overgrown garden. At the bottom of the garden was a tree house covered with ivy and weak, old, wet wood. The people who lived in the cottage were Lisa and James, the two children, and their mother and father.

One morning James and Lisa went to their tree house. In the tree house was a pencil pot, paper, dominos and snakes and ladders.

That night as Lisa went to bed, she looked out of her window, where she saw a white thing with two black, dark eyes staring at her! She thought it was a ghost, but it was best to forget about it and go to sleep.

In the morning, her and James went to the tree house and the ghost had left a strange-looking, small horseshoe. She touched it and her hand went through it. It took them both to another place.

There was a donkey waiting for someone to ride on him, so they jumped on his back. It took them to another wood. Suddenly, their long-lost dog came jumping up at them and next to the dog was an elf. The elf knew what the ghost had been doing. They asked him and he said he had been trying to give the dog back because someone had stolen the dog and had hidden it. The ghosts came to blame it on him. They were shocked.

They decided to go back home. When they brought their dog home, their parents were surprised that they had the dog, but nobody believed their adventure.

Rhian Beynon (9)
Penclawdd Primary School, Swansea

A Day In The Life Of My Dog

There once was a dog that lived in the same house as me. Yes, you guessed, he is my dog.

One day he went on an adventure in the house. He was sleeping in his cage, when he heard a sound. He ran upstairs when he heard the sound again it was coming from my mum and dad's bedroom. He went in, he had never been in my mum and dad's bedroom before.

He jumped on the bed, he had never been on a bed before. He started to jump on the bed and he did a backflip. Then he heard a noise from my bedroom.

The teddy bears were having a teddy bears' picnic, so Bo joined in. Bo had a biscuit in the shape of a dog. That night he had nowhere to sleep. Bo asked the biggest teddy bear, 'Can I sleep on you?'
'Yes, you may,' said the bear.
'I will have to be off in the morning,' said Bo.

The next day Bo found out what the sound was. It was my brother squeaking his squeaky toy and that was the story of a day in the life of my dog.

Chloe Porter (8)
Penclawdd Primary School, Swansea

SHORT STORY

One day in my house, I was watching TV. Oh hello! My name is Rachel and my brother and sister's names are Nathan and Chloe. My brother, Nathan, annoys me sometimes, but my sister, Chloe, is OK.

One day my friend Lucy came to call for me and I went out. We were walking along a path and we saw a haunted house.
I said, 'Shall we go in?'
'OK,' said Lucy.
So we did. It was freaky and scary too.
I said, 'Let's get out of here,'
'No, you said to come in, so you are staying with me, OK?'
'OK.'

So we went down this tunnel and suddenly there were two ghosts coming up. I said, 'Run!' So we ran all round the house, then stopped. But they were still coming, but we forgot that. We had a torch in our pocket. We got it out and shone it on the ghosts.
'Hooray! The ghosts have gone.'

We carried on walking until we saw a lot of people cleaning the walls. One of them was my brother's girlfriend, Katherine, and all my best friends. I said, 'Come on, before it's too late.' They all came out of the haunted house and never went in again, forever.

Rebecca Williams (9)
Penclawdd Primary School, Swansea

GHOST STORY

One day I woke up and it was still dark. I went to get my mum, but she was not there. So I went downstairs to see if she was there, but she was not downstairs either. I sat down and wondered where she was and then I heard a noise. It went, *'Ooooohh, ooooohh.'* It was coming from under the stairs.

I crept over and I opened the door. When I opened the door, there was a ghost. The ghost had my mum. My dad had gone to work. I was frightened. I got my mum back and my dad came back from work. The ghost came back and took all of us away.

Hannah Stuckey (8)
Penclawdd Primary School, Swansea

THE HAUNTED HOLIDAY

A few weeks ago, on the 28th November, 2002, I was packing my suitcases into a van to go to New Zealand. Me and my family were off. It took a while, so I was tired. I looked up and saw something. It was green and black, like a ghost.

We were at the airport but I was still thinking of the green and black thing. We got on the plane and when the trolley came around with the food, I looked up to say thank you, but the lady had gone. I shook my mum and then when I looked up again, she was there.

We landed and I was really excited. I was jumping like a kangaroo. We saw my auntie and uncle waiting to take us to their house. So they took us there and introduced us to everyone. Then I went to sleep.

I got up and I thought the ghost must have gone, but then I saw it. It was on a cereal box. I screamed and let go of the box and the cereal went all over the floor. I was going to find out what it was.

I decided the next time I saw the ghost I'd get some salt, but that didn't work, so I tried pepper. It worked and then I said, 'Don't mess with me,' like I was a hero. Then he never showed his face again.

Rhiona Williams (9)
Penclawdd Primary School, Swansea

TV

There was once a boy called Guy Davies who loved the TV. He loved it so much that his brain knew every programme at every time, even at midnight. His mother knew that he liked TV, so she bought him a TV for his bedroom. He loved it.

One evening he woke up in the middle of the night and watched the TV. Suddenly, he heard a slurping sound. It was coming from the TV, then he looked at himself and he was being sucked into the TV. Then it went blank.

Later on he woke up and he was in tangled wires. 'Where am I?' he said to an animated character, who was running by. Guy was very frightened because there were only people that he watched on TV.

His mother was very worried by now, so she looked everywhere, but there was no sign of Guy.

Meanwhile, Guy was not having fun either, sitting looking at people going by. 'I wish I could go home,' said Guy to an animated creature, 'it is really cool there.'

It was amazing. His mum could never find him and he has stayed there to this day.

Rhys Jackson (9)
Penclawdd Primary School, Swansea

GHOST STORY

One cold, dark day I woke up because I heard a very loud bump in the kitchen. I ran downstairs as fast as I could. It turned out to be the fridge that had toppled over. I pulled out the torch from my pocket, turned it on and shone it everywhere. I heard a noise at the last place that I shone it. I saw a terribly ugly monster.

I screamed and sprinted up to my room and blocked the door. The monster just broke through and everything I had blocked it with. I had no way of escape except the window, so that's what I did. I jumped out of the window and ran away. The monster jumped out of the window and chased after me. I stood by a lamp post and as he came close I jumped out of the way and he banged his head. Five minutes later he woke up and chased me again, so I started running again.

I ran and ran and ran and ran until we got to a dead end, then we had a terrible fight. Death was heading towards me, but then I remembered what he had done to me and I battled him until he was defeated. Three-quarters of an hour later he died and I was champion. After that I went home.

Joseph Davies (9)
Penclawdd Primary School, Swansea

A DAY IN THE LIFE OF DELPHINUS

Hello. I am Delphinus, a dolphin. At least, that's what humans call me. This is my normal day for the 21st century, in my Greek home waters, carrying messages for Neptune, the God of the Sea.

When I'm not working, carrying messages, I'm allowed to frolic in the foamy, sea-green waves. I have been promised immortality from Neptune. Immortality is being able to live for ever. Many humans believe that I have been turned into a constellation of stars. How silly!

To start my day, I catch my breakfast. Then I swim to Neptune's palace where he lives with the beautiful sea nymph, Amphitrite. Neptune gives me my morning messages and I set off.

I usually get some time off for lunch, unless Neptune has rather a lot of messages for me, When I have plenty of free time, my friends, Delphina and Streak, come to play with me. We always have great fun diving to the smooth, sandy bottom of the sea and shooting up into the air. When we shoot into the air, droplets of water scatter around us like diamonds.

After lunch, I go back to work. When my work day is finished, I play with my friends. Later on, I go to sleep underneath the starry night sky.

Lorna Davies (11)
Pentip VA Primary School, Llanelli

A Day In The Life Of Britney Spears

6.45	Wake up and do my daily workout.
8.45	Have breakfast and get ready to have my hair done.
8.55	Go to have my hair done at Taffy's.
10.15	Go home, change my clothes ready for my photo shoot.
11.10	Go to have photo shoot in London for my new single that I've just recorded.
12.25	Go to W H Smith to sign my autobiography that came out to the shops last Saturday.
1.15	Arrive home, just had a message from Justin.
1.25	Ring Justin back and have a chat with him.
1.55	Go to my rehearsals for the MTV Awards which I will be attending this evening.
3.40	Go home then go to Pizza Hut with my best friend, Kelly.
4.50	Go to Kelly's house, watch a movie and have some popcorn and a can of Coke. *Delicious!*
6.00	Go home and change for MTV Awards then ring Justin to see where he is picking me up.
6.55	Meet Davina McCall who is hosting it this year.
8.00	The show begins.
8.35	I am called up to win the award for the sexiest female pop singer.
9.30	Feeling good after my performance. The dance routine went well. Let's hope this is another chart success. The audience seem to like my new song.
11.30	The show is over. What a superb end to an exciting day.

Caitlin Stephens (10)
Pentip VA Primary School, Llanelli

WHO GOT STOLEN?

'Do you want to go to the park?' asked Lisa. 'I'm on the swing,' she said.

'I'm on the other side,' said Catrin.

Lisa went on the monkey bars and the rest were on the swings. Suddenly Catrin shouted for Lisa and she heard Lisa shouting, 'Help guys.'

They went around the corner and there was a man holding Lisa. They followed him to the library so they knew where he was.

They went to Lisa's house and told her mum. Her mum followed them to the library. She phoned the police and they came over as fast as they could. The man had killed everybody who worked in the library. They caught him and he went to jail for stealing people and killing. Lisa was happy that the man went to jail, but she wasn't happy that he had killed a lot of people. The police said thanks to her for capturing the man. They had been trying to get him for 2 years for kidnapping and killing people.

Lisa went on holiday for 2 weeks to Lanzarote to clear her mind of everything. When she came back, she forgot about everything and went out to play straight away.

Caryl Earey (10)
Pontrhydfendigaid Primary School, Ceredigion

SURVIVAL

'*Waaahhh!* This is fun, parachuting from a plane!'
Crash! Bang! Wallop!
'D . . . Dad are you OK?'
'Yes! But a bit stuck.'
'I'll help you.'
Tom found a stone so that he could cut the parachute. 'Nearly there, just a bit more. *Wah,*' *Crash!* 'Oh no, nearly got it that time.'

A week later, Tom's dad died of starvation. Tom started to cry. He didn't know how he was going to survive. Where was he going to go? Would he see his family again? Tom fell asleep.

He woke up and had a walk around in the jungle. He saw many animals hiding in bushes and sleeping in trees. He saw a couple of snakes, koala bears, monkeys and some baboons far away in the distance.

It was getting dark and things were becoming creepier by the second. *Bang!* '*Owww!*' Tom crashed into something hard. *Huh, this can't be a tanker,* Tom thought. He decided to sleep in the tanker because there could be rations in there and some weapons as well as clothes. He was right.

The next morning Tom started a shooting range. He nailed *Five* on a tree and brought out a moving target and started to practise.

That night, he went out hunting for food because he had run out of rations. He caught a baboon which tasted disgusting, but as he was so hungry, he ate mercilessly.

As night fell, Tom fell asleep but was woken up by drums and singing. He started to worry. The door of the tanker started to open. He saw a white glowing ape and a glowing snake. They attacked Tom. Tom pulled out a gun and fired, but the bullets bounced off these mysterious animals and hit Tom.

'Thomas Morgan, you were fiercely attacked by the gods of the jungle, but now have no fear because you are safe with me. You are in Heaven.'

The next day, Tom's body was found and was buried in the jungle.

Joshua Davies (11)
Pontrhydfendigaid Primary School, Ceredigion

THE BEST JOURNEY EVER

3, 2, 1, blast-off! Into the unknown, Captain Chris and his brave soldiers and his crew set off to where no man had been before.

They set off on a course to the planet, Saturn. In the first hour of warm-up speed, they passed the moon then the passed the red planet, Mars. After a couple of hours, they passed Jupiter.

Early the next day, they sighted the planet the had been looking for, Saturn. When they got closer, they could see that the planet was heavily guarded, so Captain Chris sent out the soldiers to make a hole in the defence lines so that he could land his spaceship on the surface of the planet and rescue Princess Amber Brown from the ugly, spotty aliens.

When they landed on the surface, the soldiers fought their way through the underground corridors, until they came to a large chamber with five doors. Behind the first door, there were soldiers. Behind the second door, there were two ugly, spotty aliens having an argument. Behind the third door there was a mother changing her baby's nappy, and, behind the fourth door, there was an empty classroom. But, behind the fifth door was Princess Amber Brown. They managed to escape to the spaceship and back to Earth at top speed.

Gwyndaf Owen (9)
Pontrhydfendigaid Primary School, Ceredigion

THE TALE OF THE HORRIBLE ZOMBIES

Tom woke up on a nice and sunny day. He and his friend decided to go to the graveyard which wasn't far from Tom's house.

Tom had a sister called Emily. Ben and Lisa were their cousins and Ben and Lisa were brother and sister. They all met up at Emily's house. They started walking to the graveyard. They took the two dogs with them. One was called Zoe and the other Sam.

They arrived at the graveyard. First they decided to see their nana's grave. After that they were running about and the dogs were barking. They went behind the church because they heard a noise. There was blood everywhere!

They went in and all of them shouted, *'Argh!'* And the dogs were barking. The zombies and ghosts were chasing them. They were chasing them around the place.

Finally they went home. Even the dogs were scared. They all agreed never to go there again. They thought it was a dream. They didn't tell their mums and dads. They didn't tell anyone.

Two months later, they told their mums and dads about the story. They decided to return but there was nothing. There was no blood on the windows. There was nothing there! It was weird. They told their friends and they went there. They saw exactly the same thing! They thought that when their mums and dads go, the ghosts and zombies don't come out. But when the children go there they see them. Their plan is to kill every child.

Cerian Davies (10)
Pontrhydfendigaid Primary School, Ceredigion

THE BOUNTY HUNTER'S DAUGHTER

Today was a great day for a hunt to defeat a space pirate called Bongru who was a very, very strong man. He was always wearing a blue and black martial arts suit with a dragon on the front and back.

'Lunega, come here and cut the hair off my tail!' demanded Leigh.
He was a bounty hunter. He was the one who wanted to capture Bongru once and for all, after two thousand years!

There was no reply from Lunega, Leigh's daughter. There was only the sound of the hot wind of Leigh's planet hissing through the windows and doors.
'Lunega!' cried Leigh.

Lunega had gone to Rughliu, Bengru's home planet along with the other space pirates. Leigh was really mad. He jumped into a jet and went off to Rughliu with Zigu, his best friend.
'Hi Leigh, how are we going to destroy Bongru?' asked Zigu.
'I will destroy him in hand to hand combat. He will be evenly matched,' replied Leigh.

After arriving, ninety ninjas came out of nowhere and killed Zigu, but Leigh avenged Zigu and killed the ninjas with brute force! Then, amazingly, Zigu regenerated and went up to Bongru's castle. Zigu had a bad time defeating Bongru so Leigh stepped in with the galaxy police as back up.
'Argh!' screamed Lemma and Gofocks as the two galaxy police officers got sliced in half by Gotnna the head of the 'G' ninjas and Letta, the second best space pirate alive.

Leigh had a fierce battle with Bongru, but then Leigh struck Bongru with a sword and killed Bongru forever.

After heading back home, Leigh had his tail trimmed by his rescued daughter, and that night Lunega and Zigu got married.

Guto Morgan (11)
Pontrhydfendigaid Primary School, Ceredigion

Noooo!

A long, long time ago, a little boy called Timmy was walking down to his next class. Something scared him, but it was only the builders.

Timmy, Lucy and Jo were very excited because they had just moved up to their new school.
'Isn't this exciting?' said Jo.
'Yes, but I am scared because of all the older people,' answered Lucy.

One day, before the summer holidays, Timmy was walking down the hall when he heard a voice. Suddenly he saw a ghost hovering in the air. Timmy was shocked. 'Who . . . who are you?' asked Timmy.
'Why, I'm Sir William Pen, who are you, little boy?' asked Sir William.
'Timmy,' he replied.
By this time it was dinner break.
'What are you doing here, Timmy?' asked Sir William, and he made a silly face to make Timmy laugh.
'This is my new school, Sir,' he answered.
Just then the bell rang for in time.
'Oh well, I have to go. See you later,' shouted Timmy, and, as he said it, the ghost disappeared.

After Timmy's lesson, he went to see Sir William, but this time Sir William was not so nice. He had a knife in his hand!
'Why have you got a knife in your hand, Sir?' he asked.
'I'm just going to use this knife to kill you!'
'Noooo!'

Katie Watson (11)
Pontrhydfendigaid Primary School, Ceredigion

SHEILA'S ALP

Sheila's Alp was very quiet until Rhyno clones started appearing and Sheila was captured. Three goats escaped, Billy, Pete and Ralza. They freed Sheila so now it was time to kick some butt!

Chapter 1

Sheila was by a river. Over the river were some clones, their eyes were dark red. They had horns that glistened in the sun. Billy, Pete and Ralza stepped back a pace and started whistling. Sheila got the gist and jumped over the river. The clones charged. Sheila jumped again, they all banged heads. Sheila muttered, 'Oh, oh,' but then the goats charged and *poof,* they disappeared.
Billy said, 'Why, thank you. Now I'll go home.'
'Okay Billy,' said Sheila.

Chapter 2

Pete shouted, 'My home, my home!'
His face fell. Rhynos were cloned out of giant toadstools. They looked angry. Pete said, 'Give them a left and right, Sheila!'
Sheila snuck up a toadstool then down again and kicked hard. It fell over. She did it with all of them and then made the Rhynos disappear.
'Thank you, thank you, Sheila.'
'No prob Pete.'

Chapter 3

A big water moose had Ralza cornered. Sheila jumped on its back, it was like a bucking bronco. Then it smashed into a wall and went *poof.*
Ralza said, 'Thanks, Sheila, I thought I was a goner. Here, have these boxing gloves, just in case any more come. Bye Sheila. See ya soon!'
'Yeah! Bye Ralza!' said Sheila.

__Hannah Phillips (10)__
__Pontrhydfendigaid Primary School, Ceredigion__

A FAMILY'S MYSTERY

One night there was a sound, a sound that scared Elinor, Gwen, Crystal, Mom and Dad. It sounded like a cry or a scream for help. Everyone knew that something mysterious was going on!

The things that made the noise were a dog and a little girl. Elinor, Gwen and Crystal didn't know why. They heard the cries for help so they went to find out. Then they wished they hadn't because they saw a man with a knife who cut the little girl's hand off for some reason. It was very puzzling.

Elinor found a book in the library that said, 'There is a man cutting people's hands off for a spell'.
'Gwen, Crystal, I've solved the problem. The reason he's cutting people's hands off is that he's trying to make a spell!'

When they found him in their doorway, they phoned the police. They came right over and took him to jail.

Crystal Bartholomew Biggs (9)
Pontrhydfendigaid Primary School, Ceredigion

A DREAM COME TRUE

Everybody has dreams, for some people their dreams won't come true. Let me tell you about a little girl who had a dream and worked really hard for it to become reality.

It started like this. Kate was an average twelve-year-old girl, but she had a very different dream to most girls. She wanted to be an astronaut.

One day she was reading through a magazine and she saw a competition asking for her to design a rocket. The prize was to go to NASA and to go into the rockets.

A few weeks later, she had a letter through the post telling her she had *won!* She and her family could go to America.

When they arrived, Kate was excited. She went to bed straight away because she was so tired. But the next morning Kate was very ill. She had caught the flu and she had to go home.

Twenty years on and Kate has been working on a project with NASA to find life on Mars. Kate's made a machine and it finds water on Mars. When Kate finds out, she phones her best friend up immediately and tells her. Soon the whole world knows. She is now one of the most famous people in the world, and her mum and dad are really proud.

Tanwen Davies (11)
Pontrhydfendigaid Primary School, Ceredigion

THE MYSTERIOUS STONE

Let me tell you about the mysterious stone . . .

It was 500 BC. There were two little boys called Peter and Mark. They lived in a very poor village. The two boys and the rest of the village were starving to death because the country was too hot! No plants were growing as food, and there was no rain!
'Peter, we've got to do something about this,' said Mark looking desperate.

The next day was the hottest in the country's history.
'Mark, I can't cope with this anymore!' said Peter feeling angry.
That afternoon, something strange happened. The village, usually very quiet, was unbelievably crowded with people.
'Mum, come here, you won't believe what is happening out here!' screamed Mark.
'What rubbish are you . . . *wow!*' said their mother.
Mark saw something shine. He went to look at what it was. It was a powerful stone with words written on it, saying, *This Is The Mysterious Stone.*

Bethan Davies (11)
Pontrhydfendigaid Primary School, Ceredigion

THE CHOCOLATE STREAM

When the world was unusual, two boys were walking and suddenly one boy saw something like mud running along by his side. 'Look,' said the first boy.

'Wow, what is it?' asked the second boy.

'It looks like chocolate or something, doesn't it?' said Tom, the first boy.

They were lucky enough to have a bottle with them to take it home.

As they were walking home, they were talking quite a lot. Once they were home, they told their parents and their parents said they should do something with it.

'We should sell it in pots and we'll have a lot of money,' said Billy. 'After we've sold it, we will have around £2,000 if it sells.'

'We should start on the market tomorrow at eight o'clock sharp.' said Tom.

Early next morning, Tom and Billy got up very early to go and get the chocolate and put it in pots. After they put everything ready and took it to the market and started, there weren't many people coming. But, in the afternoon, a lot of people came and bought a few pots of chocolate and called it chocolate spread.

A few weeks later, they were millionaires! They did a lot of things with the money like buying a bigger house compared to the old little house they lived in. They went on holiday and bought a new car and they were rich, all because Billy and Tom found the chocolate stream.

Rhiain Davies (10)
Pontrhydfendigaid Primary School, Ceredigion

CAT CALLED AMBER

One day there was a little boy called Tomos. Tomos had a little cat called Amber. Amber was a naughty little cat. Amber killed a lot of birds and rats.

One day Tomos woke up and peered out of the window to see if Amber had gone out during the night. All he could see was Amber killing a bird and a rat at the same time. He rushed down in his boxers and shouted at Amber, 'Leave that bird alone. Kill the rat instead.'
But Amber didn't listen and the bird went.

When Tomos went into the house, he felt sick. His mum and dad told him to go to bed and that he would feel better later. So Tomos went to bed. When he woke up, Mum had put Amber back in her shed. Tomos could see the door wide open. He went out to whistle, but Amber didn't come. He ran into the house to tell Mum, Dad and Nanny that Amber wasn't in the shed! 'I'll go down the path, Sid you go to the river. Dad and Mum will stay here.'

Tomos found Amber crying in the skip with a cut on her back leg. He took her to the shed and went to bed. He woke up in the morning, went to the shed and found Amber was dead. Tomos was heartbroken.

Tomos Lewis (10)
Pontrhydfendigaid Primary School, Ceredigion

THE BEST DAY OF MY LIFE - MY FIRST KITTEN!

When I went to the sanctuary, I didn't know what kitten I wanted. I thought at first I wanted a ginger one, but he was very wild. I stood looking around, staring at all the animals. I could not choose. I leaned back, tired, on the cage behind me.

Suddenly I felt a wet feeling on my finger. I turned around and it was a tiny black and white kitten. I shouted out loud, 'That one, that one!'
I took the black and white kitten home excitedly.

I named him Patch, yes, Patch! Patch can be naughty sometimes. He killed a bird and brought it into the house to my bed. We didn't let him out for a day! Sometimes he follows my sister when she goes to bed.

Patch is the best cat in the world. Patch is the king of all cats.

Gwen Thomas (9)
Pontrhydfendigaid Primary School, Ceredigion

COCONUTS

On an island in the middle of the Atlantic Ocean there lived a monkey named Coconuts. The island was also called Coconuts because of all the coconuts on it. Coconuts (the monkey) loved eating coconuts and that's why he was called Coconuts.

One day, he and his monkey friends were having lunch, coconuts for Coconuts and palm leaves for his friends when they heard screaming on the other side of the island. The scream was from Mike.

Mike was ten years old and always wanted to fly in an aeroplane. Today he had hijacked a space plane at his local airport. He couldn't control the plane and it had crashed onto Coconuts. Mike had screamed because he had seen all the monkeys on the island, but now he had calmed down.
Coconuts walked forward. 'Um, welcome to Coconuts, how are you?'
'Argh! He can talk!' screamed Mike.
The other monkeys started muttering about Coconuts talking to a human.

Mike went into the half smashed plane to phone a friend who worked in a circus. While he was phoning, Coconuts told his friends that when he was born, a spell was cast on him so that he could talk in any language.

In ten minutes, another plane landed and a man came out of it and said, 'Which one spoke, Mike? Was it him?' pointing at Coconuts.
'Yes,' said Mike.
The man grabbed Coconuts and put him in his plane. They flew to the circus and lived happily ever after.

Lucy Morgan (10)
Pontrhydfendigaid Primary School, Ceredigion

LOST LAMB

Little lamb was forever wandering off - after all, the world was such an exciting place to explore.

'Little lamb,' said her mummy, 'you must stay where I can see you. Otherwise you might get lost or get into trouble.'

But little lamb wasn't listening. She was too busy chasing rabbits or playing with frogs in the stream.

One day, little lamb spotted a big blue dragonfly hovering over the water. She chased after it, skipping across a stone bridge to the other side of the stream, but she soon lost sight of it. When she looked around, she couldn't see her mummy anywhere either. As she crossed the little stone bridge, she looked over to the other side. Her mummy was stuck in the stream with her foot in-between the stones. Quickly little lamb called her friends and together they pulled her mummy free.

'I'll never wander away again, Mummy,' she said.

'Just look at the trouble you get into without me!'

'Sorry for wandering off like that.'

'That's OK!'

Kayleigh Chandler (10)
Pontrhydfendigaid Primary School, Ceredigion

NIGHTMARE INN

Hey, my name is Kenny. I've just been waiting for my mini laptop to boot up. Right, my parents just sent me off to a freaky old inn called Night Inn, but on the sign, someone had scratched mare after the *Night,* so now it read . . . *Nightmare Inn!*

'All on for number eleven!' shouted the bus driver.
When I got on the bus, I realised I was the only passenger on the whole bus. 'Where has everybody gone?' I asked nervously.
'Nowhere, because everybody knows that the Night Inn is haunted!' the driver said shakily.
'Hau-haunted?'

The bus stopped outside the inn. At first I started to explore the place, it was freaky but not as freaky as inside. *That* had scrapes down the wall as if someone had let a cat in. The driver was right - it was haunted. He said something about no one wanting to go there.

A week later, I started to explore the rooms in case someone wanted to jump out at me. I went this way, that way, turned a corner and I was lost. 'Hello, is there anybody out there?' I shouted.
'Go away!' said an angry voice under the door.
'Who is there?'
'Jamie Oliver,' he said calmly, 'you are in great danger. At ten o'clock tomorrow night, I will become a werewolf. If you stay any longer I might eat you.'
He must be joking, I thought, but I thought wrong. I ignored him and stayed.

Joshua Dower (11)
Terrace Road Primary School, Swansea

THE COOLEST DAY ON EARTH

As I was walking from the shops, I saw a shiny thing in the middle of the road. I picked it up but people stated to chase me. I was starting to beat them up.

I got out of the alleyway and a silver Aston Martin caught my eye. A man stepped out and said, 'The name's Bond, James Bond.'
Then he took some kind of gun out of his pocket and shot a line of fire in front of the people. 'Jump in,' he ordered me and we raced off down the street.
I showed him the shiny thing and asked him what it was. He said nothing. As we were driving on the motorway, he said, 'You're on a mission now.'
I heard a beeping noise that sounded like a phone and a screen popped out of the dashboard. On it was Head of HQ. She said, 'There's something going on in the old church in China Road. You'd better go and check it out.'
So we did but it was only workmen who were demolishing the church. We headed back to the mansion.

The next morning we arrived at HQ. M said, 'There are people trying to steal the crystal.'
We checked it out - they were hanging from the ceiling. I shot an arrow to cut the wire. They fell to the ground and more people burst through the door. They surrounded us and started to hit us and kick us. We threw gas bombs. (We put gas masks on.) One of the men had the crystal but we grabbed it and ran to the car. James allowed me to drive.

As we were driving, they were gaining on us. I pressed the turbo button. We got out of the car and shot a rocket at their car which blew up and we returned the crystal to the museum.

We went back to the mansion and he gave me a medal and said, 'You're an agent now.'

Dalton Morris (11)
Terrace Road Primary School, Swansea

Bob's Great Adventure

On my way home one evening, I decided to take what I thought was a short cut. As I reached the entrance to the dark alleyway, I began to feel exhausted at the thought of running up that long and very steep hill.

It was very hard to begin with, but the light at the top of the hill inspired me to move on. Seconds later, I heard a roaring sound and, before I could get out of the way, I was swept back down the hill by a flood of water.

I was thrown out of the alleyway and landed in a heap on the grass. I lay there stunned, wet and very cold for what seemed like hours. As I regained my senses, the warm sun on my back filled me with new hope. I said to myself, 'I *will* climb that hill.'
I returned to the entrance feeling very determined. I began to run like I had never run before.

Eventually I reached the top of the hill to be met by a loud shriek which came from an enormous giant. The giant picked me up in its huge hands. I lay quite still hoping my life would not end like this. I found myself flying through the air and landing with a thud on solid ground. I ran like the wind to escape the giant.

When I was safe in my home, I said to myself, 'A spider's life is a hard life.'

Sean Knox (11)
Terrace Road Primary School, Swansea

THE HELPFUL GHOST

'1,000,000 bottles of beer on the wall, 1,000,000 bottles of beer, you take one down, pass it around, 999,999 bottles of beer on the wall,' sang the voices of the pupils of Nexus School for Gifted Youngsters.

'I can't believe it, we're really going to Hydro Quest, it's been my dream,' Hembert explained as if it had been his lifelong dream and had only opened yesterday.

'I don't really like water. Water's cold, wet and, well, water!' complained Frank.

'Uh, Miss Dorey, there's supposed to be a turning here,' said Burther, the bus driver.

Every child on the bus held his breath as if the class hamster had just died.

'Oh Burther, you've been holding the map upside down the whole trip!' huffed Miss Dorey.

'Prove it!' snapped Burther.

'Oh yes, north always points down, doesn't it?' said Miss Dorey, sarcastically.

'Well, we'll need to stop in the next town or we're going to be hitch-hiking as we're out of petrol!' shouted Burther.

'What about this town, it's called Deserted, population 0,' asked Hembert.

'Looks like a nice quiet place,' said Miss Dorey as if she had been born yesterday.

'Everybody out,' yelled Miss Dorey.

A strange noise flew through the air.

'Did you hear that?' asked Hembert suspiciously.

'Hear what?' replied Leeroy.

'Argh! What's that?' screamed all the children.

'It's a *g-g-ghost!*' shrieked Miss Dorey with chattering teeth.

'Hi, I'm Alfred, I just came over to see if you were OK.'

'Yeah, we're fine, but we could do with some petrol, Alfred,' said Miss Dorey.

'Here's some petrol, it's from the cars that were left when their owners saw me,' Alfred said whilst handing over the petrol.

'Pardon me if I'm being rude, but shouldn't you have loads of ghosts with you scaring us off?' asked Hembert.

'There aren't any more ghosts. I'm the only one left. It gets lonely here so I take every chance I get to meet new people,' explained Alfred.

As the children left, they tried to shake Alfred's hand and thanked him. 'Don't tell anyone what just happened because no one will believe you,' clarified Miss Dorey.

And the children of Nexus School for Gifted Youngsters went to Hydro Quest and got wet in happiness and yes, Alfred did too.

Toby Adamson (11)
Terrace Road Primary School, Swansea

A Day In The Life Of My Cat

'That was a nice sleep,' yawned Christopher as he drooped out of his room. 'Ah, stupid cat!' shouted Christopher as he fell down the stairs. 'Ow my . . . tail! Ah, I have paws, hey, I'm my own cat!'

'Christopher, breakfast!' cried his mum from downstairs.
'What am I going to do? I know, I could go to the kitchen and through the cat flap. It's risky but . . . here goes, nothing.'
Christopher ran straight for the kitchen having no idea what lay ahead.
'Well, I could get used to this life, wait a minute! If I'm in my cat's body, then my cat must be in my body! Never mind, she is smart enough.'

Meanwhile back at the house, Mum was getting suspicious.
'Christopher, you're acting strangely,' said his mum looking puzzled.
I'd better go home, hey, what's happening, get off me! thought Christopher.
'Shhh!' whispered a voice.
'Miaow!'
Christopher had scratched him.
'Oh my stomach!' I'd better get home quickly.'
'Tabs - we've been looking for you for ages,' panted Christopher's sister.
'Miaow, miaow,' cried Christopher desperately trying to tell them how much pain he was in. We'd better get you to the vet,' said his sister anxiously.
'And quick,' added his mum.

They sped to the vet as fast as they could.
'Vet, vet, something has happened,' screamed his sister.
'OK, bring him here,' said the vet.
'Christopher, don't go in there!' yelled his mum.

Ahmiaowbuzz (big changeover noises).
'What happened?' asked his mum.
'Oh nothing,' replied Christopher
Everything was back to normal.

Jessica Hughes (11)
Terrace Road Primary School, Swansea

SPIN THE BOTTLE!

'My turn,' said Pixie grabbing the Coca-Cola bottle and spinning it.
It landed at Nick's feet.
Pixie's face lit up with an idea. 'I dare you to go up to that derelict house and stay there for a whole ten minutes.'
As she said this, Nick got up and started to walk calmly to the (what people called) *haunted house on the hill!* After a minute or so, Colin, Louise, Luke and Jenny started to follow.
'Come on, Pixie, it'll be fun!' cried Luke from halfway up the damp hill.

Pixie rolled her eyes and started to follow. When all of them had got to the front door, Nick banged on the handle which was in the shape of a lion's head. It opened automatically. All six of these eleven-year-old children walked into this house. Were they scared? They were petrified, but that didn't stop them.
'It's a bit gloomy here, isn't it? Wow, look how many staircases there are,' cried Luke in amusement. 'Let's see what's at the top!'
As he said this, he started to walk up the first staircase. None of the rest of them wanted to follow, but they knew that they couldn't let Luke go there on his own.

They walked up and up and up until all six of them heard footsteps coming from the room above their heads. They all ran down the stairs to the front door but it slammed and locked in their faces. A black figure walked slowly down the stairs, reached inside his pocket and . . .

'Extra, extra! Six children have gone missing. Last seen playing spin the bottle on a pavement!'

Florry Austin (11)
Terrace Road Primary School, Swansea

IS IT THE END OR JUST STARTING?

Jody Anna Sullivan, who is 14, lives with her mother, Susan Sullivan (32) and her dad, Fred Sullivan (33).

Jody couldn't get to sleep one night and heard a loud rattling at the window. When she looked out of the window she saw a very pale face fade into the tall dark trees in her front garden. All she thought was that she was imagining it but she got to sleep after that.

On the following Friday, Jody was reading her book on her bed and all of a sudden the electric went off. Her mother was in the shower and shouted from the bathroom, 'Jody will you go and check the power switch for me?'
Jody replied back in a worried voice, 'OK Mum I'll be back in a tick.'
She got to the shed. Having forgotten the keys, she ran back into the house. Jody searched and searched for the keys in every way possible. As she went out the back to the shed, the keys were in the shed door. The tip of her fingers were about to touch the switch when the electricity came back on. She was unspeakably spooked. She went sprinting into her house as fast as possible, locking every door which she passed and went back on her bed to read her book. After a minute or so the power just went but she wasn't going back out to the shed.

She started to look around because the power didn't seem to come back on. As she lifted her head up to look on top of her coloured cupboard, she saw extremely evil eyes, with the pupils as dark as the colour black could be and a mad mixture of yellow and green for the veins. Jody screamed loud, louder and louder still. Her father came in to find her empty bed with the covers all over the place as she had had a dreadful struggle.

Ashleigh Nicholls (11)
Terrace Road Primary School, Swansea

HOTEL HORRORS!

As soon as I, Rebekah Davies, entered the gates of Hotel Horrors, I felt a weird shiver crawl up and down my spine. Not the spine-chilling feeling the leaflet said we were supposed to have, but the spine-chilling feeling of doom.

I entered the hotel with my three best friends, Emily Peters, Florry Austin and Leah Davey. We all have our own personalities like, Emily is the fashion-bound slayer wannabe, while Leah is the amazing tap dancer, but she's the chatty one. Florry is the talented author to be and me, well I don't know what I am. Anyway, back to the hotel. I think all my friends were having the same feeling because they all threw me *the look*.

The car was probably vibrating we were all shivering so much! *Screeech* went the gates of the hotel.
'Oh my god it's so . . . so . . . scary!' said Emily.
The car stopped suddenly and an old man walked up to our car. 'What is your business here?' said the strange man.
'Uh, a trip,' I replied.
'What trip?'
'A trip,' Leah said impatiently.
'And you're visiting the house?' he asked.
'No . . . we're staying in the house,' said Florry.
'That would not be a good idea,' he said, 'no one has stayed here and lasted the night.'
'Uh, I think we should go home now,' Florry said.
'No, he doesn't scare me and he's meant to scare us!' said Leah.
'If you wish,' muttered the man.

The wrought iron gates opened and as they shut behind us, the man laughed and said, 'They'll never get out!'

Rebekah Clement Davies (11)
Terrace Road Primary School, Swansea

A Day In The Life Of Me

Hi, my name is Olivia Head. I had a brother called Tom and my mum's name is Kathy and my dad's name is Graeme. We all live at 44 Terrace Road. We are quite an ordinary family really. My mum works in her clothes store, my dad works as a welder. *But* there is this one girl called Shumain she's so horrible she bullies me every day after school.

It all started one day in school when Mrs Mreca called me to her desk to see my work but Shumain pushed in front of me, but Miss didn't notice, she just said to her, 'Is this the best you can do?'
'Yeh, why?'
'Look how neat Olivia's is compared to yours.'
Shumain never ever forgot that day. She bullied me every day after that.
'Hey Olivia, where you going?' That's what she said every day after that. For two years she bullied me non-stop and said she would kill me if I told anyone. After all that bullying I got a bit sick of it so I began to take a different route home from school but she found me out and it was even worse than before.
'Trying to get away from us Olivia?' she said.
'Of course not,' I stuttered.
She kicked me and punched me and I fell to the ground.

That night I went home and my mum wanted to know where all of the bruises had come from. I said, 'Nowhere!' but she kept on about it so in the end I gave in and told her everything. She went mad and ran down to Shumain's house.
'What have you been doing to my daughter?'
'Nothing honestly!'
'Tell me the truth!'
'OK, OK, I have been bullying her for a while but that's it. That's it, that's it.'

After that Shumain never bullied anyone again. She was scared of me for a while but I made sure she wasn't by making friends with her, eventually.

Olivia Head (11)
Terrace Road Primary School, Swansea

GHOST TRAIN OF DOOM

'Shanade are you ready? Hurry up, we have to go and get the others,' shouted Jack.

'Be quiet,' said Shanade.

'You know what she's like, doing her hair, making sure she looks alright for all the boys,' replied their mum.

Finally Jack and Shanade went to get the others. They were really excited about visiting the fair, so were Kelly and Matthew. They all promised that they would go on the ghost train three times. Laura only had enough cash for one turn.

They got to the funfair.

'Wow, look at all the wonderful rides!' Matthew said in surprise.

'Well come on then let's go on the ghost train,' yelled Kelly.

Laura said, 'I will go on the last turn which is the third turn. Go on, you go on it now, I'll have the fun of hearing your screams!'

Shanade, Jack, Kelly and Matthew went on twice. They thought it was absolutely brilliant. Laura finally went on and sat on her own, while the others sat in front. They went through the doors. All the others weren't scared but Laura was a bit nervous. The next minute, *bang!* Laura screamed, 'Argh, help, some kind of gooey man has got me.'

'Stop playing tricks Laura,' replied Matthew.

The cart stopped. All of them screamed. 'Argh.'

'Laura, Laura, are you OK? Don't worry, just don't move,' whispered Shanade.

'*Roar!* You get me out of here or else . . .'

Shanade screamed, 'Argh!'

Kirsty Jayne Bell (11)
Terrace Road Primary School, Swansea

WOLVERINE'S REVENGE

'I'm not an animal, I'm a man!' Logan screamed as the thugs advanced on him. Getting out his claws, Logan killed the thugs and went to find the professor who put metal inside him and turned him into an animal known as the Wolverine.

Logan ran inside the lab. Just then an alarm was sent off and thirty thugs ran into the lab and started shooting at Logan. Logan jumped, grabbed the leader, broke his neck, picked him up and threw him at some test tubes. Boom! As the test tubes mixed they exploded, killing all of the thugs. Logan grabbed a thug and dragged him to a handprint security system. 'DNA accepted,' the computer said.
'Don't come any closer,' the professor wailed, 'you're just a dead man.'
'Can a dead man kill?' Logan said.
'You know I injected you with a lethal disease,' the professor replied.
'How long do I have?' Logan asked.
'Normally one year, but with your mutant healing ability I don't know.'

Ten years later Charles and Michael were discussing Logan's disease.
'Michael, how long do I have left?' Logan asked.
'Two days,' Michael replied.
'Two days?' Logan screamed. 'But that's my birthday!'
'You'll have to go and see my old friend Craig, he'll know what to do,' Professor X said. 'Storm will fly you to Craig's hideout.'

'I've been expecting you Logan,' Craig bellowed.
'Give me the serum or else!' shouted Logan.
'Or else what? You'll stab me with your weak little claws?'
'Aaahhh!' Wolverine screamed as Craig grabbed him with his powers, but Wolverine bent down, picked up a piece of iron and ran towards Craig and killed him. Wolverine grabbed the serum and injected himself with the cure for the disease.

Lloyd Breeze (11)
Terrace Road Primary School, Swansea

UFF MAWL'S REVENGE

Wolverine and Spider-Man were hanging out by the beach. Silver Surfer was surfing as usual, when Pyro their next-door neighbour rang on Spider-Man's mobile to say a few people had broken into their mansion. Spider-Man told Wolverine and Silver Surfer what had happened so they all zoomed off. Wolverine on the motorbike stolen from Cyclops, Silver Surfer on his surfboard and Spider-Man on his webs.

When they got back to the mansion it was wrecked and their rivals stood united. Spider-Man faced his rival the Green Goblin, Wolverine faced Sabretooth and Silver Surfer faced Magneto. All of a sudden they burst into a fight. Magneto held Silver Surfer still with a magnetic field. There was no hope; he couldn't move as Sabretooth bit him with poisoned teeth. Spider-Man spat a web at the Green Goblin's eyes but he used a powerful poisoned gas in return. One man was left, Wolverine, but not for long, he was killed by a blast to the neck from Sabretooth.

They thought it was all over, until he came! A loud Uff Mawl came bursting through the door. Uff Mawl told them that he was Wolverine's brother and it was time for revenge and with one powerful beam, all three were killed. Uff Mawl used his powers to revive Spider-Man and Silver Surfer but he couldn't revive Wolverine. He cried a tear and whispered, 'Sorry brother.'

Ever since that day Uff Mawl, Spider-Man and Silver Surfer have been The Silver Heroes, saving the solar system from evil.

Thomas Adams (10)
Terrace Road Primary School, Swansea

JESS AND THE FLYING LOBSTERS

Once there was a boy called Jess. He was walking home from school, on the path in the park. Suddenly he saw something shiny glittering on the grass. He ran to it and saw that it was a crystal shining in the sun and then as soon as he picked it up a sudden urge of fear came over him. He ran home with the crystal in his pocket, unaware of the powers inside.

That very night the crystal lit up the whole room and started swirling around, changing colour. Jess woke up and saw the flashing lights then he got sucked up into the crystal as it if was a time portal.

It took him to the Planet X where there were two different kinds of beast (one is the flying lobsters; the other is very strange, it is sort of half shark and half human). But Jess did not know that this world was already owned by the beasts!

Jess was walking along what he thought was a cliff. As he was looking over the edge he saw what he thought to be movement below the mist and then he saw the shark-like figures rising from the mist! Jess took a step back, but nearly fell off the cliff as they drew closer, inch by inch. Suddenly the ground started to shake as the cliff flew into the air. Jess was speechless but as soon as they took flight, he woke up and found out it was a dream.

Grant Wilshere (10)
Terrace Road Primary School, Swansea

THE RETURN OF THE MASTER

It was a quiet night in Sunnydale and Buffy Summers sat on top of a gravestone in the cemetery. She seemed bored, flicking her stake in her hand. She was waiting for Giles to meet her.

'Hi Buffy,' said a voice. 'It's me!' called the voice, it was Angel.

'Don't creep up on me!' she cried.

'Sorry,' Angel said quietly.

'Why are you whispering?' asked Buffy.

'I need to tell you something . . .' he answered.

'Let me guess, I'm in danger.'

'I wish I had better news,' he whispered.

'Tell me!' said Buffy loudly.

'Last night I found a book which held a ritual . . .'

'Hello!' Giles had arrived.

Buffy went to turn around, as she did her face turned white. There were vampires digging up the spot where she had poured away the master's bone dust.

'Let me do this guys,' she said. She spun around to face the vampires.

'You're mine, slayer,' one laughed.

'Well if I'm correct . . .' she kicked him across the face, 'it's the other way around.'

He tried to hit her back but missed. Buffy looked around and saw another vampire running away with a jar of powder. Buffy pushed her way through the vampires and ran after him. She chased him all the way through the cemetery and back to the spot where he had been digging. The vampire tripped, Buffy grabbed the jar and ran home.

When she got there, she slammed the door and sprinted up the stairs. She threw the jar out of the window and flew back down the stairs. She opened the back door and started to throw earth at the jar. Buffy then burst into tears of relief.

Emily Peters (11)
Terrace Road Primary School, Swansea

THE STORYTELLER

Dylan Jacobs was completing his new book called 'Imagination'. A couple of days later he decided to read it to a gang of teenagers who lived down the road, but he had no idea the characters in his book would come to life.

As he was reading to Dawn-Amelia (known as DA) and her friends, the book rose in the air and the fictional characters, Sedric, McLay the assassin, Cliffe Rodric the murderer, Chloe Redric the bomb maker and Jay Chandler the guy who was supposed to be a zombie, jumped out of the book and ran through the door.

'We're going to have to run after them!' shouted Romeo, DA's best friend.

'You can't!' said Dylan Jacobs. 'If they see you Chloe will blow up the world!'

'What do you mean? You're coming with us!' screamed DA.

'What, do you mean us DA? No way, the rest of us are coming with you!' wailed Shalimar, Romeo's sister.

After an hour of arguing, the group of teenagers decided to run and find the deadly adults. Finally they caught up with Sedric, Cliffe, Chloe and Jay in The Royal Bank.

'I have an idea,' suggested Samantha, DA's 5th best friend. 'We can corner them in the back room and scan them into the computer!'

The teenagers quickly put this plan into action and the characters were gone forever.

Leah Davey (11)
Terrace Road Primary School, Swansea

GAVIN THE CREEPY GHOST

Once there was a ghost called Gavin living in the Caprice Woods. The ghost was indeed very freaky and if anyone was in the woods at midnight he would sing really creepy songs and maybe perform some of his bloody tricks.

One day a boy called Tom was in the woods at midnight and little did he know there was a ghost around. As the boy was just passing by the ghost's hideout, he was suddenly pulled into a dark and silent room. Poor Tom didn't know what in the blue was going on so he tried escaping. It was no use, the doors were locked, the windows were locked! Tom was absolutely terrified. He shouted, 'What do you want whoever you are?'
There was no answer. He shouted again and the ghost said, 'I don't want anything except you and your blood!'

Tom kept trying to escape but the ghost was always in his way. He was extremely horrified. Finally Tom saw a man with a piece of wood. Quickly he tried distracting the ghost whilst the man came from behind and tried to burn the ghost. However, before he could do it the ghost killed the man. Luckily the man killed the ghost at the same time.

Tom quickly sprinted as fast as he could to get out of the freaky wood. When he was just about to get out someone grabbed him from behind and pulled him backwards. I wonder if it was another ghost?

Bilal Miah (11)
Terrace Road Primary School, Swansea

CRITICAL GAS HOBOS

May 28th, 1999

It all started on an ordinary day in May at Easefil when someone released some Critical Gas from their chemicals. Throughout the city everyone was infected. The police arrived to discover that everyone was a hobo zombie. The police shot them with pie guns but the hobo zombies chewed the police up. It was over for Easefil!

June 2nd, 1999

Five days later a special SWAT team entered the chewed to pieces city, where they found chewed bodies. The SWAT team members: Bison, One Leg Man, Pencil, Queez and The Pork, found survivors and a whole army of hobo zombies walking towards them, wanting to chew them up.

Pencil tried to kill them with a carrot gun but he got chewed too much, so his rubber came off. Then The Pork opened a door and hobo zombies pulled him in, grabbed his head and began chewing on his face. All that the SWAT team could see was a hand sticking up. The team climbed on top of the president's White House and stole a helicopter and escaped, except One Leg Man who stayed and got gassed to death by Critical Gas. The city was ruined by Critical Gas Easefil.

Steven Van Duinen (11)
Terrace Road Primary School, Swansea

MIDNIGHT DOOM

'I knew this was a bad idea,' moaned Jenny as she trudged through the leaves.

'Stop whining,' snapped Colette, 'it's only for one night. Plus, no one ever comes in here.'

Ellie, Terah, Brandon, Colette and the two sisters, Paige and Jenny, were going on an adventurous camping trip in the neck of the woods. How could their parents let them sleep in the woods all night, without an adult, without a phone? Well, in fact they hadn't.

After they'd found a spot to sleep and set up their tent, it was time for sleep. Everyone crept into their sleeping bags and slowly drifted off to sleep.

Ellie woke with a start. Something had disturbed her, but she couldn't figure out what it was. She heard it again. It was a slow scuttle of leaves behind her. The noise moved towards the tent entrance and a shadow appeared in the form of a puppet.

'Argh! Guys!' Ellie shrieked.

They all jumped up and immediately changed their clothes, as Ellie told them about the puppet.

'Are you sure you didn't dream it?' asked Brandon, as he opened the tent.

'I'm sure. It had a knife too. I have to kill it.'

'Can you say *over-reaction?*' taunted Terah.

'Can you say *blood-sucking chest wound?*' Ellie taunted her back.

All of a sudden, Ellie tripped, falling down a hill and pulling Brandon and Terah with her.

'Ow,' they chorused slowly. They got up gradually and realised that Colette and the twins had not followed.

Where are they? Terah wondered.

Right there in front of them lay the bodies of their friends.

'Oh my god,' said Ellie in disgust.

One by one they fainted and the puppet shadow appeared again, peeling the skin off each of them and putting them into his mouth.

Carla Wood (11)
Terrace Road Primary School, Swansea

TALES FROM PARADISE PARK

In Paradise Park there are swings, a see-saw and there is a pond with beautiful fish. The creatures who look after the park are Skipper and Skeeto. Skipper is a mole who wears blue shorts, a white top and a red cap, he has a cute little nose. Skeeto is a mosquito who wears blue shorts, a blue top and a blue jacket. Skipper cleans the paths if they're dusty and Skeeto whizzes around to see if anything has happened.

One day, when Skeeto was whizzing around, he saw a cat on the ground looking around. Skeeto knew who it was, it was Scratch Cat, he was part of the witch's gang, so Skeeto rushed to the garage to tell Skipper about Scratch Cat. When he told Skipper they searched all around in the garage to find something that would scare Scratch Cat. They went with a sheet on them because they would look like a ghost but Scratch wasn't scared. Scratch said, 'Come closer my little friends.'
'That's it,' announced Skipper and he pulled out a little clockwork dog which he had taken from the garage. He wound it up and *zoom,* it went after Scratch and he ran away.

The next day, another terrible thing happened, the wicked witch was zapping everything. Skipper was just about to play on the swings when he noticed that they had melted. Skeeto had noticed the same thing, he had been by the beanstalk tree and it had melted too.

They both went to the garage to find something that would scare the witch. Then they heard a cackle so they raced outside and there was the witch flying on her broom, trying to zap Skipper and Skeeto, but they were dodging. Skipper quickly saw a big stone and threw it at the witch. The witch fell and died and Paradise Park had brand new swings to replace the melted ones. They lived happily every after.

Emma Rainey (10)
Terrace Road Primary School, Swansea

THE GHOST AND TWO GIRLS

In an ordinary classroom there were two children, their names were Kelly and Jennifer. Kelly liked sporty things like swimming, football and running. In football she supported Liverpool, she was a fan of Michael Owen. She also liked sweets, but not too many and she hated Pizza Hut and chocolate and sprouts and mushrooms. Jennifer was fourteen and a half. She liked the opposite things that Kelly liked, except for sweets. She liked girls and boyfriends. She also hated mushrooms and sprouts.

The classroom had two tables and chairs and two computers. They had just been given a pile of work with no instructions at all. They just had themselves.

It was play time. They weren't allowed to go out, instead they sneaked out to the hall. The hall was large and had a stage at one end and lots of doors leading to classrooms. They had never found it spooky before, until they heard a noise. It sounded like '*Ooooo.*' They just thought it was an owl sleeping. Then they heard it again, they were scared this time, it sounded like '*Ooooo, I'm coming to get you! Come out wherever you are!*'
The ghost was white. The ghost said, 'I want to be your friend, I won't kill you.'
Do they die or not?

Carla James (10)
Terrace Road Primary School, Swansea

THE MAGIC NUMBER

Jack had had a bad day, he had tripped over a massive, silver, shiny stone. On the floor he found a magic rubber, but he did not know that yet. 'I wish it was a magic rubber,' said Jack, 'I would rub out that stupid stone that I tripped over and hurt my leg and knee.'
He threw the rubber at the stone and something very strange happened. He could see the stone disappear into thin air.

He ran to tell all his friends about this whole magic story. Together, they all decided to rub out something else. However, when they got there they saw that the rubber kept changing colour.

They kept the rubber and whenever they saw something dangerous, they would rub it out.

Amir Hussein (10)
Terrace Road Primary School, Swansea

THE MIRROR

Once upon a time, far away, there lived a widow called Mary. She lived in a dark mansion. One day she went up into the attic and saw a mirror. It was dusty. She blew the dust away. On the frame it said: *Whoever looks into the mirror will be swapped with the person in the mirror.* Mary didn't believe in it and looked into the mirror and was sucked into it.

A hundred years passed. One night when a family were going to their house, their car broke down. They saw the mansion. The door was open. A girl called Angela Mary Thomas started exploring the mansion. She went up to the attic. There she saw the mirror. For some odd reason there was no dust and no cobwebs. The same warning was there. Angela got her brother, Dale. Dale was scared. After all he was only eight years old. Angela said, 'Who cares? It's only a mirror.'
Dale said, 'But what if it's cursed?'
'Don't be stupid,' said Angela. She looked into it. She was sucked into the mirror just like Mary. Then suddenly another Angela came out but she was opposite. Angela had a clip on her right but this Angela had one on her left. This was freaking Dale out.

Now the only one who could stop the opposite people was Dale. Everything about Angela was opposite. In tennis she hit with her left instead of her right. Dale was thinking really hard. He got his sling shot and broke the mirror. What happened next? Find out!

Joshim Uddin (10)
Terrace Road Primary School, Swansea

DARK CLOUD

In a village far, far away, there lived a boy called Snape. He lived with his mum. One day he went to a festival and was watching everyone dance. Elsewhere, the Dark Genie was awakened from a four-hundred year sleep. He was in the mood to destroy villages. He was above the village where Snape was. He was dancing with his girlfriend, Page.

At nine o'clock the genie attacked. Everyone ran, a windmill was falling. Snape ran towards Page because she had hurt her leg. The windmill fell. There was a flash of light, the fairy king appeared. He gave Snape a magical stone where he could get Atler. Atler was a ball with a shield which only he could break. He said that he put everyone and everything in one. There was a flash of light and Snape was back in the village. He went to a cave called Diving Beast Cave. He was on the eighth floor when he found a cat and some transforming potion.

He took the cat home and his mum said, 'Do you want to keep this cat?' 'Yes,' Snape said, 'her name is Rose.' Snape went to play with Rose but she was sad. He gave her the transforming potion and Rose turned half cat, half human.

Later, Snape returned to the cave and on the fifteenth floor he found Dran. He knew Dran had a spell on him to make him bad. Dran charged, Snape dodged. Snape jumped on Dran's back and hit him twelve times with his sword. The spell stopped. Dran gave Snape a lift out of the cave. Snape said goodbye to everyone and went on to save the world from the Dark Genie.

Michael Davis (10)
Terrace Road Primary School, Swansea

A MOON ADVENTURE

The space camp were going to the moon. This was a day I would never forget. Jenna, Lucy, Scott and I were getting ready for lift-off. All of us were so excited, we thought of the long journey through space. We would be floating and spinning on the moon. Beyond ourselves, we all had different thoughts on what it would be like out there. Maybe we would see a burning meteor or a comet. After about two or three minutes our thoughts were destroyed by the yelling of, 'Lift-off!' We got ready, held on tight and hoped things would go well.

Up in space it was fantastic. There were many silver objects floating and we were as well. Beyond the darkness, a flash of lightning appeared before us. We were very, very calm. It was so fascinating, it was like a play area.

Later on, we decided to go for a walk, we did not want to go together so we decided to go our different ways and started to look for unusual objects. I was really enjoying myself, it was brilliant. After a while, I headed back to the spaceship, but there was one problem, I was lost. I panicked, then suddenly an alien appeared!

The alien spoke English. 'How do you do?'
I was speechless, it was a live alien. After a while we got used to each other. I understood the alien wanted to help us.

Lucy was the first to find me, we were planning with the alien to find Scott and Jenna. Now Scott had found Jenna and found the spaceship. Then the alien found the spaceship with Scott and Jenna beside it, so that meant we were all together again.

It was not long before we were ready to leave. It was a long journey home, but we made it. Everyone was happy for us. It was certainly a worthwhile visit!

Lucy Evans (10)
Ysgol Cynlais, Swansea

LOST IN SPACE

'3, 2, 1, ignition, blast-off!' It is the first Welsh mission to space. This was to be a special day in my life. Stephen Ellerby, Cara Isaac and myself from Ystradgynlais and Miranda Burdette from Abercrave were all travelling on *Roced Cymru* to space.

'This is very exciting,' said Stephen, when we were just approaching space.
'Yes it is very exciting,' I said. 'I wonder how long it will take us to get to the moon?'
Then suddenly a noise came from the radio. We thought somebody was going to tell us something; sure enough someone was talking to us. The control centre said, 'Congratulations, you are now in space!'

A few hours later we were approaching the moon and we landed on the moon carefully. Then we got into our spacesuits and walked on the moon's hard surface. There were special radios in our spacesuits so we could communicate with each other.

Then, as quick as lightning, we saw a bright red flash and we realised that somehow we had been taken to the dark side of the moon. We knew it was the dark side of the moon because we could not see Earth.

'We have been taken to the dark side of the moon,' said Miranda in amazement.
'That means we are lost,' Cara said.
At that moment everybody felt scared, even Stephen.
'That means we are far away from food, drink and our spaceship,' I said, while my teeth were chattering and my legs were wobbling.
Then Cara screamed, 'Argh! Look over there! It's an a-a-alien!'
There, in front of us, was an alien. It had two eyes on stalks and two small arms with three bony fingers. The rest of its body was like a slug's and it was a mossy green type of colour. Then it spoke to us. 'Do not be afraid we will not hurt you. We have brought you here to help you.'
'You mean there are more of you?' said Stephen.
'Yes,' the alien said.
'What shall we call you?' asked Cara.

'You may call me Crater. First you must come to our city and have food and drink,' said Crater kindly.

'Oh yes we would like to have food and drink with you,' I said (and I said to myself, *hooray!)*

The alien led us into a deep, dark crater and we went inside. There were lots of long tunnels with lights in them. We walked until we came to a row of homes all brightly coloured, orange, yellow, pink, lime-green and many more colours.

'Wow,' said Miranda, 'this street is very colourful!'

'Yes, the lime-green house is mine,' said Crater, 'it's very pretty isn't it.'

'Oh yes it is very pretty,' Cara said happily.

Then Crater knocked on the door.

'Yes?' said a voice.

'It is me, Mum,' said Crater.

'Come in dear. Who are these things?'

'They are people and their names are Bethan, Stephen, Cara and Miranda and they come from the planet Earth.'

'Are you joining us for supper? We are having cushacoo plant and jusoflam.'

'Yum, yum,' said Crater.

A few minutes later, we ate our food and it actually tasted nice.

'We must hurry,' said Crater.

So, very quickly he led us to a cave. In the cave were lots of precious stones that glittered in the light.

'You must choose three stones,' said Crater. He spent half an hour explaining about the stones. We chose Peace, Happiness and Love. Then there was another red flash and we were in our spaceship.

A few hours later we were back on planet Earth and everybody was happy and everyone loved each other. From that day on there was no more war. We were presented with medals of honour the following day and we all lived happily ever after.

Bethan Ellerby (9)
Ysgol Cynlais, Swansea

LOST ON THE MOUNTAIN

Amy Littlewood was on her way to her friend Graham's house. She was tall and pretty with dark brown hair and sea-blue eyes. She was generous, kind and always cheerful. Graham was short, he had light brown hair and grey eyes. He was funny, full of fun and never stopped smiling.

When Amy arrived at Graham's house, he suggested that they could go hiking on Mount Gabriel. It was very sunny and they didn't plan to go too high up. When they got to the mountain they started climbing. Neither of them noticed the weather changing.

Eventually they found a path so they started walking along it. Suddenly a flash of lightning appeared in the sky and a blizzard started. They were both very frightened. Graham noticed a cave where they could hide for shelter, so they ran inside.

It was icy cold so Amy started to make a fire. After a couple of hours the blizzard died down. They ran outside to find that everything was covered in snow!
'Where is everything?' asked Amy.
'I don't know,' replied Graham, 'but I do know we're lost!' He was right, they were lost and it was getting late.

Amy had an idea, she built a fire and collected as many stones as she could. Graham was confused, he had no idea at all what she was doing. About half an hour later she showed him her SOS sign. She had made it right next to the fire so that any passing planes or helicopters could see it.

They sat by the fire for hours hoping to see a helicopter, but they didn't. It was one o'clock in the morning and Graham said, 'Let's just give up, we're never going to be rescued!'

Just at that moment, a helicopter landed! They were escorted on to it by two rescue men. They were discussing their experience when Amy said, 'I don't know about you Graham but I'm never going hiking again!' And neither of them ever did.

Francesca Linton (11)
Ysgol Cynlais, Swansea

THE MYSTERIOUS CELLAR

'I won't be long. Whatever you do, don't go into the cellar,' whispered Mum into Tom's ear, as she gave him a loving hug.
'Why not?' asked Tom curiously.
'It's cold and dark down there and anyway, you might be scared, it's pitch-dark,' she replied. She gave Tom one more hug as she set off.

Tom walked to the window and waved her off. As soon as she went, he ran through the kitchen, past his computer room, past the cellar . . . Tom stopped and walked backwards. Did there just come a groaning voice from the cellar?

Tom wondered whether he should just stick to what he wanted to do. Should he go and see if Dragon Ball Z was on? Then there was another groan, even louder than before. Tom stared at the knob on the door, eyes wide open, full of curiosity. He touched the knob then drew his hand away as if it was on fire. Tom then had a whirlpool of questions filling in his head. What's down there? What's making that noise? Is that not the real reason why Mum didn't want me to go down there? A loud wailing groan brought Tom back to Earth.

Tom decided to go down, he lit a candle and made his way down the creaking stairs. As he entered the cellar at the same time the groaning got louder. In the end the groaning got so loud that Tom knew where the groaning was coming from. He carefully opened the coffin-shaped box and inside was nothing but a mummy.

'Aarrgghh!' screeched Tom as he ran back up the stairs - the mummy followed. The mummy chased Tom through the house even though the mummy was ancient and stiff, he always caught up. Tom began to realise that he needed to get rid of him and without thinking he grabbed one end of the wrappings of the mummy and began to unravel it.

'I'm home, did you miss me?' Mum called.
she took off her coat and went into the kitchen where she found Tom and the wrappings of the mummy.
'Tom, what did I tell you about playing with the kitchen roll!' she shouted.

'It wasn't me!' he exclaimed as if he had been arrested for a crime he didn't commit. 'There was this mummy, and he . . .'

'Enough of your baby stories,' she said, 'now go to your room.'

Later on Tom started not to believe it himself. Had it really happened?

Katrina Klein (11)
Ysgol Cynlais, Swansea

LOOK WHO'S TALKING!

One beautiful morning in Florida, the crystal clear waves with joyful dolphins leaping out of them, gracefully washed up magical shells onto the golden sand. Ashley's bedroom looked straight out onto this magnificent sight.

Amy was woken by a short bark as her three-month-old Springer Spaniel named Bob, leapt into the room and rushed back out again to wake her brother Ashley. The two met on the landing and went downstairs to have breakfast. As they got into the living room there was a flash of brown and white when Bob rushed through first.

After breakfast, at about ten-thirty, the twins and Bob of course, went out into the back garden to play ball. The ball flew high into the air as it went from Amy to Ashley - Ashley to Amy. Bob was getting a bit frustrated.

'Just give it to me!' bellowed a high-pitched voice, 'now!'
'Who said that?' asked Ashley.
'Me, Bob!' muttered the dog angrily, 'j-j-just give me the ball!' he said, looking up at Ashley.

They all carried on playing until their mother called them in for food. Ashley and Amy explained this weird and quite unusual thing to their mother. But she didn't think that they were telling the truth because after lunch all four of them went into the garden to do the same thing again.

On September the first, a month after Bob spoke and four months after Bob was born, Amy and Ashley were out in the garden throwing the ball for Bob. When suddenly Bob spoke again.

So in went the twins to tell their mother and later on Bob was packed into the cage which they'd had when they bought him. When they got to the vet, the vet checked him over and asked, 'Is Bob the oldest dog out of the litter?'

'As far as I know, yes!' spoke Amy shyly.

'This is a common thing,' explained the vet, 'all the oldest pups can talk, so everything is fine!'

Anna Lewis (11)
Ysgol Cynlais, Swansea

MOON MURDERS

It was the year 3012 and Tim Daultry, Buzz Altron and Max Smith entered their glistening rocket at NASA launch pad. They were about to have the holiday of their lives. This superb supersonic rocket roared as there was lift off. A tremendous heat was distributed, displaying a vibrant glow at its tail. The lights sparkled like diamonds and beautiful gemstones. The rocket sped through the clear, starry sky as fast as a bolt of lightning.

At last they had reached the moon. The atmosphere was electric, full of excitement! Silently the rocket door glided across. The highly trained astronauts floated through the atmosphere. An eerie silence greeted them. The mist was as thick as candyfloss. They investigated this empty world with great caution, keeping together as a team. The massive porous rocks covered the ground. Bright illuminous, green water trickled and bubbled over the rocks and formed into murky streams. The fizzy water frothed like limeade pop as it formed into a bubbling murky river. Acrid vapours steamed like a boiling pan. Ragged waves floated into an ocean of froth like the top of a cappuccino coffee.

Suddenly there was a bone-chilling roar and a gruesome monster appeared from behind a rock. It had jagged, clamp-like teeth, four bulbous eyes and its body was covered in a tough coat of scales. Sheer panic took over! The astronauts feared for their lives.

Max Smith motioned towards a huge, dark crater. Slowly they drifted towards it, each second of time feeling like a year. The gruesome being tailed close behind, breathing a hot, rancid breath. A powerful force pulled the astronauts inside and spun them around like an out of control fairground ride! Death was instantaneous. The evil source had its prey and the devilish monster exterminated these strangers. Satisfied with this result, it continued to patrol this unknown world where no one was welcome.

Jordan Briskham (10)
Ysgol Cynlais, Swansea

THE ORPHAN GIRL'S NEW FAMILY

Once there was a girl called Kelly, she was an orphan and always hoped for a mum and dad.

At the orphanage she would sit at the side of her bed every night and pray for a family. Then one miserable, damp and cold day, she was called to the headmaster's office.
'Don't be scared, you're alright, come on.' Kelly went in, Mr Davies, the headmaster had some good news for her.
'Kelly, you were promised to have a family, the Morris' are kind, funny and really generous.' But what he didn't know was that the Morris' were really nasty, mean people and they tortured children with the belt and threw them into a dungeon and left them there. All the children had was a bed, bread and butter and water.

Kelly packed her bags and caught a taxi to the Morris' house. After unpacking she could screaming coming from the walls. She asked Mrs Morris where the screaming was coming from and she told Kelly it was just the wind!

After lunch, she heard the screaming again, she got suspicious and went to investigate, *where it was coming from?* She moved the curtain and found a passageway, she went through, it was deserted, with bones everywhere. She came back to find Mrs Morris sitting on her bed with a belt, about to whip her. Suddenly, just before she started to whip her Kelly's real parents came bursting through the door.

'Kelly, we've been looking for you everywhere,' they said.
'Mum, where have you been? You left me all alone to be put into an orphanage!'
'It's a long story, come on, hop in the car and you can come and see your new house, because you're coming to live with your dad, brother Zack and me.'

Sophie Smith (11)
Ysgol-Y-Castell, Kidwelly

A DAY IN THE LIFE OF SAMANTHA

Hi, I'm Samantha (but you can call me Sam). I should tell you about myself - I have two best friends, Carly and Tracy, they are so cool. Once Carly climbed into Mr Jin's garden (Mr Jin is the most horrible man in the world, I'm telling you), Carly was chased for miles and Mr Jin had his Rottweiler too and his Rottweiler is just horrible, even though I love animals. Guess what he calls his dog? It's Buddy. He says to it, 'Come on Buddy, let's leave these kids', and he spits on the pavement. I think he's horrible, fat and ugly. Well let's get off this subject *completely.*

My mum's name is Karren and my dad's name is Bill. My mum works in a shop and my dad works as a builder. Shall I tell you how many animals I've got? 35! I'll tell you what I've got, right! I've got 5 guinea pigs, 10 newts, 5 rabbits, 2 goats, 5 dogs and 8 fish. My animals are hard work, I can tell you!

I hate school, especially my teacher Miss Big Bottom, actually her name is Miss B Biro but she's got a big bottom, so I call her Miss Big Bottom. The thing I also hate about school is our break, we only get ten minutes in the juniors and in the infants, they have half an hour! Is that fair? I don't think so! I also hate Mrs Quibble the IT teacher. Every time I accidentally type a word wrong, there's a shout in my ear.

It's time to say goodbye, I've got to go - my mum's calling.

Rosemary Harris (10)
Ysgol-Y-Castell, Kidwelly

AMBER RETURNS

Amber is a psychic cat. She is of the darkest black and quietly moves in the shadows of the night. Her coat is sleek and her eyes are the colour of amber.

She targets people she doesn't even know, though she always knows exactly where to find them.

One dark night when the moon was full and the lightning raced and danced in the dark, navy blue midnight, Amber discovered she also had the power of invisibility.

All winter her new target had been an innocent young girl by the name of Kelly.

Amber slipped gently out of her tree and along a garden path. She knew that in this very house, the cold, dark, gloomy house lived her target, Kelly. She walked up the wall to Kelly's bedroom and using her psychic powers she opened the window, Kelly woke with a start but all she could see was a pair of brilliant orange eyes staring down at her from the ceiling. Kelly let out a high-pitched scream but it was too late, the eyes were plunging down towards her and they then disappeared. Kelly ran to her parent's bedroom and shouted, 'Amber returns!' But Kelly only felt a piercing pain in her back as Amber leapt at her and sank her vicious claws into her.

So from the hole in the tree in which she had been scared to . . . Amber returns!

Josi Spiccelli (10)
Ysgol-Y-Castell, Kidwelly

28 DAYS LATER

In the dead of night, graveyards can be spooky, especially when mad doctors come out to play.

One day, a boy named Frank was playing, when his mother called him to go to the doctors. Frank was worried because he doesn't like doctors; in fact, he hates them because he's really scared of them.

So off he went to the doctors. He walked into the room and the doctor grabbed him. The doctor wasn't like any doctor he had seen before; he was a funny colour and had a funny smell.

Frank was more scared than he had ever been in his life. The doctor tied him up and kept injecting him with very sharp needles, which made him go to sleep. He tried to fight back but it was not good enough.

After 28 days, Frank found himself in the back of a van and when it stopped there was darkness all around him. He was pushed out of the van and managed to get his bandages off. He was in a spooky, quiet graveyard and he ran and ran until he was tired and fell to the ground. When he woke up someone was shining a bright light in his face. It was a policeman who told him that he'd been missing for 28 days and everyone was looking for him and the doctor, he was called Doctor Frankenstein.

The policeman took Frank home and Frank's mum promised not to take him to the doctors again.

Richard May (11)
Ysgol-Y-Castell, Kidwelly

A DAY IN THE LIFE OF A FISHERMAN

It was raining last night but today it's a bright, sunny day, perfect conditions for fishing. Bob woke up early, 6 o'clock and he decided to go sea fishing. He had already prepared his tuna sandwiches, roast beef crisps and four chocolate bars the night before. He took with him in his fishing bag, small and big hooks, colourful floats and a spare line just in case it runs out. Weights for ledgering and a lantern so Bob could fish throughout the night. Bob also took sand, eel bait and a waterproof tent.

Off he went down to the seaside. The tide was out so Bob had quite a walk. He gathered his fishing gear and he set off. There were plenty of other fishermen along the water's edge. Bob chose his spot and began to set things up. The rod was cast into the sea. Bob knew it could be a while before a fish rose to his bait so in the meantime Bob got out his foldaway chair and fishing magazine.

Just then, Bob's rod began to bend and the line started to unravel, He leapt up off his chair and struck, then he played the fish. Eventually he reeled in a double figure bass. Bob put it in his cool bag to keep it fresh and cast off again. Bob thought his first fish was just a bit of luck, but no! Altogether that day, he caught five bass, six flounders, two jellyfish and of course an old boot.

He thought he'd caught enough for the day so he decided to have an early night ready for more fishing tomorrow.

Rebecca Evans (11)
Ysgol-Y-Castell, Kidwelly

HMS INVINCIBLE

One foggy day, HMS Invincible came into the harbour. My dad Richard was on board; he's in the Navy.

My mum and I walked on to the ship to look around. My dad took us all around and we saw lots of things that were interesting and which I didn't know about. We met Dad's mates with their children and wives on board.

After looking inside the ship we walked outside to look at the helicopters, there was one helicopter with tiger stripes on it. We saw the pilots on board and Dad introduced us. We went to Dad's room to have a drink and after that we went down the corridor to look at all the pictures of the ships, helicopters and submarines and all the people on board ship. They have been everywhere on that ship, but on Friday 29th May, my dad retired after 24 years in the Navy. He wasn't on the ship for 24 years because he went to Bosnia for six months.

When he finished in the Navy we had a party and Dad gave out presents to everybody. He had a lovely 24 years in the Royal Navy, but it is nice to have him home with mum and me.

Megan Mattey (11)
Ysgol-Y-Castell, Kidwelly

THE MYSTERY OF LIFE

Crash! Bang! Smash! Craack! A tree had just fallen by the two wrestlers in the sky, the howling wind was like a wolf calling, the moon and the lightning was making quick, sharp, gleaming shots upon the house which everybody and everything feared.

I dare tell you what happened, the thought of it makes the hair on the back of my neck freeze solid and sends a shiver down my spine. *Suddenly* a croaky old voice and a faded shadow came from a dark alleyway. A crowd gathered to listen. It was an old man but when he came closer our bodies became paralysed. Our mouths hung open wide and our eyes hooked onto the old man.

'I'll tell you what really happened,' said the old man, 'I was the gardener of that house until it happened.'
'Where have you been all these years?' asked the crowd curiously.
'I was simply gardening when a horrific scream met my ears, I rushed in the house and I simply died and I've been in slavery ever since,' the old man said.
'You what? Bbbuuuttt that means you're a ghost!' the crowd said in horror and before the crowd could do or say anything, the old man's eyes turned dark, dark red. It was like looking into Hell! Instantly the crowd shattered . . .

Florence Hamilton (11)
Ysgol-Y-Castell, Kidwelly

MONSTERS FROM HELL!

'Zzzzzz!' snored Jessy as she lay in bed.

Smash! went the vase in the hallway and Jessy woke up. She found herself running in to her brother Jimmy.
'Jimmy! Jimmy! Did you hear that smash?' whispered Jessy.
'Go away, I'm trying to sleep,' said Jimmy as he turned over.
Then they suddenly saw something move through the gap in the door.

'Come on, let's go and find out what's going on!' said Jimmy as he got out of bed. They quietly tiptoed around the house looking for any strange creatures, lurking about.

'Argh!' screamed the children.
'Argh!' screamed the werewolf.
'Quick, grab a knife, anyone!' shouted Jimmy holding his hand out. He took it from Jessy's hand and stabbed the werewolf and it fell to the ground.

A ghost and a vampire heard the screams and came to the killing scene.
'No! A vampire and a ghost! What are we going to do?' shouted Jessy.
'Quick, grab a stake!' bellowed Jimmy, 'and stall the ghost!'
Jessy handed him the steak.
'No, wrong steak, oh well . . .' he pushed the steak towards the vampire's heart and said, 'It's true, red meat can kill you! Now pull the ghost apart.'
'Okay.' *Rriiip!*
'He's dead, let's go and tell Mum and Dad.'
'Argh!' screamed the children.
'You killed them, now we will kill you!' said Mum and Dad in a croaky voice. Dad took out a knife and struck twice. Both children lay dead on the floor.
The parents cackled and said, 'That's the end of them! Ha! Ha! Ha!'

Claire Sullivan (11)
Ysgol-Y-Castell, Kidwelly

MEGAN AND LLINOS AWAKEN FROM THE DEAD!

One night when Lauren was playing in the park next to the church, Lauren heard a strange noise coming from the graveyard. Two ghosts were playing tag. They came over to the park and Lauren asked them who they were, they replied Megan and Llinos.

Lauren was so frightened she ran as fast as she could to her home. Lauren had nightmares again but her parents wouldn't believe her so she went out for a walk on her own. To her surprise there was a haunted house which hadn't been there before.

But guess who was there? The two ghosts Megan and Llinos. Lauren was so frightened that she panicked and began to cry. She didn't want to look at the ghosts because they scared her. Megan and Llinos were calling her on. Lauren was surprised and when she shakily walked towards them.
Megan said, 'We want to be your friends, we're not going to hurt you.'

So Lauren kept the ghost friends a secret and visited them every day.

Lauren Jones & Llinos Morris (11)
Ysgol-Y-Castell, Kidwelly

A Day In The Life Of Jordan

Ow! Stop it! Sorry about that, I'm always getting beaten up by those nasty bullies. Oops, I shouldn't have said that, they're after me again. Help! All I can do is run from them. I'm only in Year 3 and they're in Year 6, I don't stand a chance.
'Jordan, Jordan! We're going home now,' shouted Mum.
'Yes!' saved by the bell. 'Coming Mum!' Jordan shouted.

'Yes! my favourite for lunch, fish 'n' chips!' Jordan cried happily.
'Eat up Jordan, no not that quickly or you'll choke. Here's some water.' (Splutter, cough, choke).
'I told you not to eat too fast.' warned Mum.
'Sorry Mum and by the way, can we go swimming?' asked Jordan.
'Okay, get your swimming kit ready and let's go,' Mum told Jordan.
'Jordan, go into the boys' changing rooms and here's a pound for the lockers,' mentioned Mum.
'Thanks Mum, I'll go in now,' replied Jordan.

'*Argh!* Not you again!' he shrieked.
'Yes, it's us again and don't try running because you'll just slip!' the bullies told Jordan.
'Gotta get changed, gotta get changed, yes changed. Now run on the mat, I won't slip then, come on now, jump in. Mum help! These boys are after me, tell them!' shouted Jordan.
'Oi, you boys, stop bullying my son!' Mum demanded.
'Ha, ha! He has to have his mum to stick up for him!' the bullies chuckled.

'C'mon Jordan, let's see your front crawl.' Mum told Jordan.
'Okay Mum. Cor, this is tiring Mum, can I stop now?'
'Okay, let's go home and you can go to bed.'
'Well we're home now and I'm going to bed, goodnight Mum!'

Sam Durell (10)
Ysgol-Y-Castell, Kidwelly

PROM NIGHT

Once there was a girl called Judy, she was visiting a graveyard. 'Why don't you come?' she said to herself.

Suddenly something jumped out behind her, her heart began to pound. 'Argh!' she screamed, but when she turned around all that was there were two boys about fifteen years old.

'Sorry, we didn't mean to scare you,' said a boy called Peter.

'Yes we did! Hello, my name is Sam.'

'What are you doing here?' Judy asked the boys.

'Well, we're looking for a grave, it says 'Judith' on it and if I was you I wouldn't be here, especially on Prom Night.'

'Why not?' asked Judy.

'They say that on Prom Night, the ghost of Judith stands waiting for her date but it is misty, so misty you can't see cars coming but all of a sudden a car came round the corner at top speed and mounted the pavement. The next day she was found dead,' explained Peter.

'That's awful,' said Judy.

'You don't actually believe that?' asked Sam.

'I don't know,' replied Judy, 'they should have some record of it in the newspapers.'

So off the children went and when they got there they started to look. Finally they got to the last newspaper. They all said together, 'Look it says here that a girl was found dead on the edge of the road, it also says that 18-year-old Ricky drove off the bridge because he was so upset about his girlfriend's death. Well that says it all. We'll go to the graveyard on Prom Night.'

Finally it was Prom Night and they all went to the graveyard and suddenly a ghostly car came. 'Let's go and see,' whispered Judy but as she turned around the boys could see that she was Judith, the ghost. They watched in amazement as she got into the car and drove away.

Chelsea Collins (11)
Ysgol-Y-Castell, Kidwelly

KERRI AND RICHARD'S ADVENTURE

One day, a girl called Kerri and a boy called Richard went out to play. They wanted to climb some trees so they went to play in the forest. They played all day in the forest and Kerri had forgotten what time she had to be home so Richard and Kerri were looking for the way out. Then they realised that they had been going round in circles. They kept on looking until Richard heard branches breaking. Richard and Kerri started to worry.

Suddenly the footsteps stopped and all was silent. Kerri and Richard kept on walking. They came to a river but couldn't get past because the river was too deep and it was flowing too fast. They saw a tree which could get them across. At last they were across. Richard said he saw a shadow. He went over and saw a dead rabbit on the tree.
Richard said, 'Someone was trying to scare us.'
They took no notice and just kept on walking.

They came to a cave and went into the cave then they carried on walking. They found a torch and saw a bit of sunshine coming through, they ran and ran and came to the end of the cave. They came out of the cave and Kerri and Richard were not late after all.

Hannah Jones (11)
Ysgol-Y-Castell, Kidwelly

THE HAUNTED GHOST TRAIN!

It all started on a warm, sunny day in Riverdale. Ashley and his parents and two of Ashley's friends were going to a fair outside Riverdale.

When they got there the first ride they went on was called Star Bouncers. Once they had come off, Ashley caught sight of a ghost train tucked away behind everything. He asked his parents if he could go on it. They said no. Ashley really wanted to go on it, so he ran as fast as lightning.

The train was deserted. No one was there but him. He walked through the dusty gate. The train was covered in cobwebs and dust. Ashley was freaked. He got on the cart and went through the doors. Suddenly a skeleton jumped out of nowhere and took him into another dimension.

He ended up on a pirate ship that was being taken over by skeletons. Ashley saw the exit and rushed to it. Suddenly he heard footsteps moving towards him and a sword slid out of its case. He turned round and saw a skeleton with a sword thrashing towards him. Suddenly he felt a sharp pain gushing through his stomach. He'd been stabbed. The skeleton marched off. Ashley crawled in pain to the exit. He fell head first out of the exit. The cut had disappeared. Ashley was amazed that the cut had vanished.

He quickly ran out from the ghost train and never went on it again!

Katy Hallett (11)
Ysgol-Y-Castell, Kidwelly

A Day In The Life Of Ian Dodd

At half-past six I wake up to the horrible call of my dad. I pull back the bedcovers and get out of bed. I race downstairs for breakfast, sit in the deep armchair and watch TV. I run for the bathroom at eight o'clock to get ready for school, then I wait outside and perhaps play for a bit until it is time to go to school. I always try and get the front seat of the car before my two brothers. I put my belt on and watch my mum reverse down the drive so she doesn't crash into the wall. As we drive I like to watch the countryside flying past, like a handful of dust put into the fans and then turned on and blown.

When I get to school I wait outside for the doors to open, then at ten to nine, everyone walks into school. I hang my bag up and run outside to play football. Year 5 and 6 normally play against Year 4. Year 5 and 6 always win. When the bell goes it is my job as captain of Castell Coch to put everyone straight in lines, to see if we can get the points from the teacher on duty.

In the classroom, Miss calls out the register and then we do work, some of it good, like science and some of it boring, like English. I like dinner time because I like to have seconds.

After school I do my homework and some nights I like to go swimming. I go to bed wondering what is going to happen the next day.

Ian Dodd (11)
Ysgol-Y-Castell, Kidwelly

A Day In The Life Of A Computer

Hello, my name is Windows XL. I live in a comprehensive school in the computer area with six others like me.

Oh no, it's Monday and silly Year 7 are on me today until break time. They've only just come from primary school so they don't know very much about IT.

'Ouch, that hurts!' They press the keys so hard to get the games. How would they like to be treated the same? They would not like it, they would be annoyed and angry.

Everyone should have respect - especially for me. They treat me like dirt every time they use me. I am sick and tired of it. They even turn me off and on and pull the wires out of my back. It hurts very much.

Mr Hopkins tried to mend me. It took from break time to dinner time trying to put the wires back in the right holes. He took a little break in the staffroom but I was trashed. My wires could not go back in the holes, so I was left all alone in the computer area with six computers all around me and guess what? They were all on except me.

Next thing, one boy from Year 7 tried to rescue me. He put all the wires back on like all the rest of the computers. I was working again, but I'm not looking forward to *next Monday* and *that class*.

Leanne House (10)
Ysgol-Y-Castell, Kidwelly

BIRDHOUSE

Hello, I am Tony Hawkes, I am the best skateboarder in the world. I am 25 years of age and I have brownish-blackish hair and blue eyes. My favourite make of skateboard is Birdhouse because when I go up the halfpipe I can do nine hundred spins!

On Tuesday I was in Los Angeles in a tournament. First I did the nine hundred spins, then I did a manual grind and then the crowd went wild! *But I wasn't finished yet*, because then I did a coffin grind and the crowd *went crazy*. They couldn't believe their eyes. Bucky Lasik was next. He was class. He was just as good as me. Who was going to win?

But then he tried to do an Impossible and then he *fell!* I had won the whole *tournament* and it was the best day of my life.

Ben Pritchard (10)
Ysgol-Y-Castell, Kidwelly

A Day In The Life Of Beckham's Teddy Bear

One day, Posh decided to take Romeo and Brooklyn for a walk. When Posh got Romeo dressed, Romeo grabbed me, his teddy bear. I've been in the family for years.

When we were on the river bank, Romeo dropped me but nobody realised that I had been dropped. I watched them going into the distance.

A few days later, I got picked up by my next-door neighbour who put me in her car. The next day I heard a child scream. It was Romeo. Brooklyn was standing right next to him. Brooklyn went in to tell Posh. Posh came out and saw me. She went into next door and asked for me back.
The neighbour said, 'Of course you can - I found him on the river bank.'

I felt so happy to be back with Romeo. Romeo was so happy. Posh didn't tell David because he would just get upset because I had been in his family forever. I really wouldn't know what he would do.

I, (the teddy bear) had a lovely warm bath and I got a lot of fuss. Romeo didn't let me out of his sight. I was so glad to be back.

Becky Harding (10)
Ysgol-Y-Castell, Kidwelly

HERO OF THE DAY

Hi, I'm Jasper, the house dog. I live in Gwendraeth Town, Kidwelly. Oh no, please don't say it's Friday. Little George is allowed out to play on a Friday.

Little George is three years old and loves dogs - but he doesn't know how to treat them. He thinks he can treat them like his toys. Then it all changed last Friday. I went for a walk down the park and George was there. He was on the swing, swinging very high. I jumped on the roundabout, ignoring him. He spotted me but suddenly he fell off. I jumped off the roundabout and ran over to George. He was breathing but not moving. He was unconscious. I licked his forehead - nothing happened. I did it again and again but still nothing happened. I ran out of the park barking at people, they didn't listen so I barked at a woman. She followed me. She saw the little boy and called the ambulance. They were there in a tick. They put him in the ambulance and took him to the hospital. I barked at the lady and she knew I wanted her to follow me to his house and she told his mum about the accident. They informed the police about it.

I was given a medal and a scrumptious biscuit, and I was on the front page of the newspaper, but the best bit of all was little George never pulled my fur again.

Emily Clough (10)
Ysgol-Y-Castell, Kidwelly

A Day In The Life Of A T-Rex

Once, a long time ago, nearly 65 million years ago in fact, back in the Cretaceous period, back in the age of dinosaurs, lived the greatest killer ever - Tyrannosaurus rex - and that's *me*.

You can call me TR, but remember that young and old herbivores should *beware* or I will kill them.

Let me tell you what happened last week. I was so hungry, thirsty and starving that I went to the river; here I would find some *food* and drink. A sound of fighting distracted me. Some predators were attacking a herd of brachiosaurus. I followed the sound and soon I found my target. There was a pack of attackers but the victims used their tails and sent them flying. They fell on me. I had food at last. I took a big chunk of meat, then suddenly something else caught my eye - a troodon had come to take some meat. I roared and chased it away. I ran back to the carcass and found that there was no meat left. It was nearly night and I had had a bad day.

Tired, thirsty and hungry, I went to bed - but now I'm recovered and feeling well because I captured a troodon and I've just picked the last bone. *Yum, yum!*

Charlie Cruickshank (10)
Ysgol-Y-Castell, Kidwelly

A Day In The Life Of A Till

Hi, my name is High Tec Till. I live in the fanciest restaurant in New England. The amount of money that goes into me each day is amazing. Now settle yourself down. I'm going to tell you about one of the worst days of my life.

It all began on a lovely day and we were very busy. People were coming and going and ordering meals, but then a lady came in and knocked me off my unit. I was so angry. I decided to get even. Cathy, my owner, picked me up and put me back.

An hour later the lady had finished her dinner, she paid £13.75. Cathy pushed my open button, but I wouldn't open. Cathy pressed and pressed until I felt I'd done enough damage for one day. Then suddenly Cathy said she had to pop out and she asked Jayne, the new waitress, to look after me.

The posh lady's bill for her caviar, salad and ice cream came to £36.00. She gave the money to Jayne, without a tip, and Jayne was so annoyed that she pressed my buttons really hard and then *slammed* my drawer shut. I screamed with pain.

When Cathy came back, she wanted to fill me with change but my drawer was stuck. She questioned Jayne to find out what had happened, and Jayne admitted she'd lost her temper. Jayne had to call out a repair man and he gave me a brand new shiny drawer - and best of all, Cathy said that only she could use me.

Megan Hyles (9)
Ysgol-Y-Castell, Kidwelly

A Day In The Life Of Gary Lineker

The day started in the same unusual way. I went for a jog, then a swim and then for breakfast. I had a ham and cheese toastie.

After breakfast, I drove to work in my S type Jaguar to Cardiff's Millennium Stadium. I was going to commentate the Premiership Cup, Arsenal versus Liverpool. It was a very important match and I was nervous. There would be many people listening. Kick-off was at twelve o'clock and the crowd was roaring.

The match began, Owen and Gerrard taking centre, Gerrard got tackled by Ashley Cole. Cole passed it to Ljunberg. Ljunberg ran, he shot and it was a goal! The crowd went mad, they couldn't believe that a goal had been scored so soon into the match. The score was 1-0 to Arsenal. Duddek passed the ball to Hyppia, Howe passed it to Rise who scored a goal and then it went pitch-black and the roof was shut. There was a power cut! The team went to the locker room and all the lights came back on! The lights went back off and then back on and the crowds started to cheer. The players rushed onto the pitch and then we found out that the match was called off.

Ryan Williams (10)
Ysgol-Y-Castell, Kidwelly

A Day In The Life Of A Kid

My story begins last Monday when I saw a woman dressed in blue jeans and a woolly jumper who was walking down the street with a baby who was full of excitement. The baby started to cry because he had thrown his bear on the pavement and his mother did not notice. I tried to tell my mum, but she argued with me.

Back in the house, my mum called, 'Josh, bed.'
'OK,' I groaned. Suddenly I heard something move. I jumped out of the window and went down the tree. There on the floor was the scariest thing I'd ever seen. The bear, alive! Then I had the guts to grab it.
'Put me down,' ordered the bear.
I dropped him. 'Who are you?' I screeched.
'I am the baby's toy and I want to get back to him. I want you to help.'
'Do you want me to carry you home?' I asked.
'Yes,' he replied.
The bear jumped into my arms and I carried him up the street.
'Left,' the bear instructed. 'Left, forward, right, left, left, right, left,' the bear said.
'Are you teasing me?'
'No, I'm just giving you directions. Just up the street now.'
By this time the bear was asleep. I carefully stuffed the bear through the letterbox and went home.

Josh Brown (10)
Ysgol-Y-Castell, Kidwelly

A DAY IN THE LIFE OF A COMPUTER

I am a computer. I live next door to Year 5 in the computer suite. There are lots of other computers that keep me company.

It was a Thursday morning and something *big* was happening. One by one, my friends were being unplugged. Oh no! Oh no! It's my turn to lose power - 5, 4, 3, 2, 1 - *blackout!*

Suddenly I was on the move. Where was I going? What was happening? I felt sick because I had not been moved before. I was pushed along the corridor, shoved through a door and then, *wow!* I was in a new room and all my friends were waiting for me. I felt a hand take my plug and put it in the socket. I could feel the energy flowing through my circuits. Oh! That felt refreshing. Next I could feel someone pressing my keys. This made me laugh.

I was in the new computer suite - and I loved it. I was going to enjoy it here!

Scott Fitzgerald (9)
Ysgol-Y-Castell, Kidwelly

A DAY IN THE LIFE OF A SCHOOLGIRL

In the morning I wake up at 7 o'clock, jump out of bed and run into the bathroom. Then I wash my hair. After, I get out of the bath and dry myself, I get dressed. I go downstairs to have my breakfast. After my breakfast, I brush my teeth. I sit down on the chair and Mammy does my hair. I go and check my bag. I go and get my trumpet and get my coat out of the cupboard. We arrive at school at 8.45. I get my pencil case, reading books and my homework, then I go to class. When we go to class, Miss will give us a mental maths test.

At 9.45, my friend and I go to a trumpet lesson. We finish the trumpet lesson at 10.15, then at 10.30 we go out to play. We come in at 11 o'clock. I go up to the desk and say, 'Miss, can I read to you, please?'

We go and wash our hands and line up to go to dinner. Mrs Davies will call us up to have dinner and do the prayer. After we tidy the plates and the bowls, we all go out to play. We come in at 1 o'clock and do craft with Miss Julie. We go out to play at 2.15. We come in at 2.45 and clear up the craft.

Ellen Rees (9)
Ysgol Y Fro Primary School, Carmarthen

A Day In The Life Of Prane The Pony

Hello, my name is Prane. I wake up every morning in a small field with lots of green trees and a wooden fence. In the spring the ground is covered with daffodils and crocuses.

My owner comes every morning and puts a rope around my neck and takes me from Annwyl and Brigwen, my daughters, to the stable where my best friend, Blackie, sleeps.

I'm on a diet so I eat lots in the field because I don't get food in the day, only a handful of something called 'coarse mix' if I'm good.

This morning was quite dull. I drank some water and chatted with Blackie about the last show she was in.

Later, when the sun was no longer shining through the door, a man called Robin came. He drove a white van and had lots of scary-looking tools. I was tied up and he scratched at my feet and picked dirt out of them. The worst thing he did was make me stand on just three feet.

After Robin left, my owner put something cold into my mouth and something heavy on my back which she strapped on tightly around my waist. Then her daughter climbed onto my back which was really awful. Finally she climbed down and my owner took off the awful things and gave me some delicious coarse mix to eat.

After they brushed me, they let me out again with Annwyl and Brigwen and I chewed some more of the fence.

Anna Bowen (10)
Ysgol Y Fro Primary School, Carmarthen

A DAY IN THE LIFE OF . . .

It all starts off when my alarm clock goes off at 8 in the morning to get me up to go to school. I get up and go and sit in the armchair and have a cup of coffee and wake up properly. My mum then puts the news on to see what's been happening throughout the night.

When I've got dressed and had a wash, I then go and sort my school bag out. Then I have to do my hair perfectly before leaving the house, because my hair can be very, very messy.

At ten to nine, me and my mum set off and walk to school.

On a Monday and Friday morning in school we have an assembly and we all either sing or play on our instruments. After our assembly we work in school and all the time we do maths in the morning and English in the afternoon.

At twelve o'clock we go up to dinner and we have so much food we are bloated! After dinner on a Tuesday we have Welsh with Mrs John and on a Wednesday we have history with Mr Thomas.

At 3.30 we say our prayers and we go home to our homes and then we stay off on Saturdays and Sundays.

Nia Evans (11)
Ysgol Y Fro Primary School, Carmarthen

A Day In The Life Of My Dog, Boyo

My dog Boyo's life starts early in the morning when my mum and dad let him out to play. When the milkman comes early in the morning, Boyo chases after the van because Boyo wants the milkman to play with him. Boyo always chases after the cats and birds.

When my sister and myself come home from school, Boyo runs up to us waggling his tail with a tennis ball in his mouth, waiting for us to throw it. When the kids come out to play, Boyo always nags them to play with him.

When it is time for Boyo to come in, he runs up the stairs like a flash, up to my mum and dad's bedroom and lies on the bed to have a little sleep, but he soon comes down for his food. When he wants some food he jumps onto the dinner table chair and just looks at my mum, dad, sister, brother and myself.

When I'm sitting down on the sofa, Boyo comes up and lies by the side of me. When everyone has gone to bed, Boyo goes to sleep downstairs on the sofa and my dad keeps a lamp switched on to keep him company so it isn't so dark either.

Abigail Carter (11)
Ysgol Y Fro Primary School, Carmarthen

A Day In The Life Of An Actress

An actress spends most of her time shooting films and shopping or having make-overs. Actresses also have a lot of interviews especially if they have a new film coming out, so it can get very hectic.

You think that actresses just do what they want all day, but you are wrong. Actresses have to do a lot of things that they do not want to do if they want to be famous.

Actresses have to go and see agents and go to charity events and they have to go to photo shoots. They also have to go to the Oscars and the BAFTAs. It can be very stressful as well because they have press, media and fans wanting their autographs. Some even have to have bodyguards and some of them have to dress up in disguise.

Of course, they have fun most of the time, going to BAFTA awards and shopping or meeting up with mates.

Actresses always go to posh or the best restaurants and being famous always guarantees them a seat. When actresses start shooting new films, they get a lot of good publicity.

It can get very hard for actresses when they are shooting films because a film can take up to a year or longer but it depends on what kind of film they are making.

Toni Evans (11)
Ysgol Y Fro Primary School, Carmarthen

My Day Out

It was Saturday and it was the summer holidays. I was going to Oakwood. We had packed sandwiches and pop to have a picnic there.

We left our house at 9am. It was a lovely hot day. When we got there it was starting to get busy. We went on the little train to get into the park. I was so excited when I saw the rides. The first thing that I went on, I was really scared but after a little while I really enjoyed it. As soon as I came off it I wanted to go back on again. The next thing I wanted to go on was the new ride, the Hydro. It looked really scary but I still wanted to go on. My mum and dad were standing on the bridge as we were coming down. They got soaking wet as the water sprayed them. All I wanted to do was to go on it again, but my mum said I had to stop and have something to eat or I would feel ill.

We sat down on the grass to have a picnic. All I wanted to do was go back on the rides. I spent all day on the Megaphobia and the treetops and the pirate ship.

Soon it was time to go home. I had the best day out I have ever had. I want to go again - soon.

Franchesca Carter (8)
Ysgol Y Fro Primary School, Carmarthen

GHOST STORY - THE HAUNTED WOODS

There were two boys walking in the woods when suddenly the ground started to move like an earthquake. The tree roots started to come out of the ground. The little tree stood there like a statue. They were so scared they could not move, some of the leaves started to come off the tree. Christmas was coming early this year. They saw some white in the distance. They ran like a bullet waiting for the kill. They could not get to sleep that night.

The next day they went to the woods again. The boys did not see anything, just footprints. They followed them. They came to a house under the ground. They went in.
'Well, well, well,' gasped a voice under the ground.

The boys came back in the dark. The same happened again. They came to the middle of the woods and something crept up behind them. It was a skeleton creeping up behind them. They could barely move. They ran home stiffly like a rusty car.

The boys came back the next day and found their friends had come out of the sheet.
'Ha, ha, ha,' they cried. 'Very funny.'
The boys gasped, walking slowly in embarrassment.

Cerys Jones (11)
Ysgol Y Fro Primary School, Carmarthen

GHOST STORY

It was ten o'clock on Monday night and I was in bed. It was freezing so I went to get another blanket. I heard a noise downstairs. I went to investigate. I tiptoed down the stairs to see what the noise was. I picked up the cricket bat and followed the noise. The noise came from the kitchen.

When I went in, something ran behind the fridge and disappeared into thin air. All was left was a letter. I opened the letter. Inside was a note. It said: 'I only appear on Mondays'.

The following Monday morning I set a trap, then I waited for the ghost. *Clash!* I had got him. It turned out to be Dad. The ghost had not come yet, I had to reset the trap. We went into the living room. The trap went again, but it was the cat. It must have been scared.

Next Monday I stayed up all night to see the ghost. That night, at ten o'clock, something came through the wall. It was the ghost. The ghost was short and fat. It had nine eyes and two noses. It had one ear. I asked it what it was doing here. It was looking for food and a home. It was lonely and sad, so we gave him a home and food and he stayed with us for a long time. He was my best friend. He came to school with me.

Emyr Bowen (9)
Ysgol Y Fro Primary School, Carmarthen

FANTASY OR REALITY?

One bright and sunny morning, Sally Trooper got out of her cosy bed and yawned. Sally was an eleven-year-old girl and had four friends. Their names were Delma, Taya, Helen and Jade. They were all normal, ordinary girls until one Saturday their lives changed.

Brring, brring, brring, brring, went the noisy phone in Taya's house.
'Hello? Taya speaking, how can I help you?' asked Taya.
'It's Helen. The gang is at my house. We are all going shopping. Do you want to come?' asked Helen.
'I'll be there in two ticks! Bye!' said Taya, putting the phone down on the phone holder.

Eventually, Taya got to Helen's house and the gang were all there, so they set off. In a matter of ten minutes the girls were in the busy heart of the town. The girls linked arms and something very strange happened. It was as if they were soaring into space. Then they vanished and went sliding down a dark and gloomy tunnel. Oh no! What was going to happen to them?

At the end of the tunnel they ended up in a beautiful place! Unicorns pranced around, gnomes danced amongst colourful houses and there were sugar and sweets everywhere! A magnificent chocolate river meandered around jelly babies who just happened to be walking around! There was just so much to take in!

Suddenly, a car made a beeping noise, it then piped up and said, ' Hello, my name is Bogus. I am your personal car. You can wish whatever you want and I will grant it for you.'
They all looked at each other and as they entered the car, Bogus made a cruel noise and laughed. He said that because they trusted him so easily, the evil people were going to destroy them. This sounded like bad news! The worst kind of news. The girls panicked and ran as soon as they saw the zombie-like creatures.
'Right, think. How did we get here?' asked Delma quickly.
'We linked arms,' cried Jade.

Automatically the girls linked arms and as quick as a flash they were transported back to town. It was as if nothing had happened. The girls went back to their normal lifestyle. Only they knew about it as they were sworn to secrecy.

Remember . . . look out . . . beware, or *it could happen to you!*

Emily Green (11)
Ysgol Y Tymbl, Llanelli

Spot The Mischievous Dog

It was the big day and Spot and the family were going to the 'Dog Of The Year Award'. Emily was so excited, she wanted Spot to win, but she knew there were bigger, better and cleaner dogs than Spot. She so wished he would win.

'Emily, get Spot, we're ready to go,' Emily's mum shouted up the stairs.
'Alright Mum,' Emily shouted down the stairs. 'Spot, Spot come here boy,' Emily said.
Spot ran from the bedroom and jumped on Emily. *Bang!*
'Spot, get off, get off,' Emily screamed. Emily pushed him off and grabbed the brush in order to brush his fur so that he looked his best.
'Emily are you ready?' asked her mother.
'Yes Mum, I'll be down now.' Emily ran down the stairs with Spot and out to the car.

At last they drove off to the Awards. This was going to be a day to remember.

When they got to the Awards, they were about to start and Spot was ready to start his mischief. He broke loose from the lead.
'Oh no!' wailed Emily's mum.
He ran everywhere, pushing the chairs over, upsetting the other dogs and terrifying the children.
'Oh no!' wailed Emily's mum.
He ran everywhere, pushing the children over, upsetting the other dogs and terrifying the children.
'No! He's going for the trophies,' screamed Emily and her mum.
It was too late. With an almighty crash they all fell to the floor. The highly polished cup, the glass bowl and wooden plaques lay on the ground in a dirty, broken pile.
'I'm, I'm so sorry,' pleaded Emily's mum. 'He's usually a placid, quiet dog.'
'Placid and quiet are not words I would use to describe *this animal!*' said the judge. 'You will have to pay for the damage!' he added.

Emily and her mum made their way out of the arena. They held their heads down low, trying not to attract attention from any more people who, by now, were all laughing and pointing.

As they opened the car door ready for a quick getaway, they heard the following words on the loudspeaker . . .

'Would the owners of Spot please return to the main arena where the judges would like to make a special presentation for the most entertaining dog of the show!'

Emily and her mum were thrilled. They ran to the arena and were greeted with loud applause!

The day had not turned out as planned but it certainly was a day to remember. Spot, the most entertaining dog of the year!

Delma Stephens (11)
Ysgol Y Tymbl, Llanelli

KIDNAPPED!

'No! Please don't go Daddy!' wailed Lauren, a ten-year-old girl with bright blue eyes and light brown hair.

Her father, a tall dark-haired man of twenty-three replied, 'I must go to help out in the war.'

'It's not fair!' cried Rhian, Lauren's nine-year-old sister.

'I'm afraid I have to leave,' her father told her gently.

Two days later a knock came at the door. It was a tall, kind-looking lady who informed them that she was called Jane and had come to look after them while their father was away. In a couple of hours their father departed.

Jane wasn't half as kind as she had appeared to be. In fact she was horrid. Lauren and Rhian were sent to bed at five o'clock without any tea or supper.

At midnight, Rhian woke up and heard footsteps. Quietly she crept out of her bed and went to wake Lauren. They were very scared. Cautiously they went downstairs. Lauren peered around the corner.

'Rhian,' she whispered, 'there are people in the kitchen. I want you to go upstairs out of the way while I go and find out what's wrong.'

Rhian hurriedly scurried upstairs.

Lauren boldly walked into the kitchen. 'What's going on?' she asked, much braver than she felt.

'Come on!' urged one of the men. 'Let's take her and go!'

'Fine,' agreed the other man. 'Jane, you take care of the other girl.' With that they rose to go.

Lauren was paralysed. She couldn't have moved even if she had wanted to.

Suddenly the men grabbed her roughly and pushed her out of the door. As Lauren was shoved into the back of a van she tripped on a rock and fell. Her head hit the van and she was knocked unconscious.

Rhian saw Lauren being pushed into the van. She opened the window and shakily climbed down the drainpipe. Just as the van was driving away, Rhian jumped on the back of the van, holding on so tight that her knuckles turned white.

One hour later, the van pulled up in front of a dark house. Quickly Rhian leapt off the van and went to hide in a copse of bushes, her heart pounding against her chest. The men dragged Lauren into the house, slamming the door behind them. Rhian sat there wondering what to do. She didn't know where she was, but one thing she was certain of - there wasn't a house within five miles of there.

Rhian jumped as the door opened and one of the men came out.
'I'll see you around sometime!' he called as he walked out. As he got into the van something dropped out of his pocket. He didn't seem to have noticed.
When the van was well out of sight, Rhian went to see what was there. It was a mobile phone so she quickly dialled the police. They came in ten minutes.

Lauren was soon saved and the man was arrested.
'What about the other man?' pestered Rhian.
'Don't worry, with him on our side,' the policeman assured her, nodding at the arrested man, 'we'll soon track him down.'

Jessica Rumble (11)
Ysgol Y Tymbl, Llanelli

THE GOONIES

The Goonies' group began when Mikey Marshal, Mouth, Data, Chunk, Brand, Andy and Tiffany met in school. They've been friends ever since.

'Hey Mikey, how's it going? Coming out today, Mikey?'

'No, not today Mouth.'

'Why not? Something wrong Mikey?'

'This time tomorrow this house won't exist.'

'Don't worry, Mickey, you'll be fine, trust me.'

Then Brand and his girlfriend, Andy, walked through the door.

'Mikey.'

'What do you want, Brand?'

'Make me and Andy some lemonade please, we're so thirsty.'

'Fine.'

'Thanks Mikey.'

'Any ice?'

'Yes please.'

After Brand and Andy finished their drinks, Mouth and Mikey were about to go upstairs.

Knock, knock, knock, there was a knock on the door.

Hello Mikey,' said Chunk, 'can I come in please? Is Andy here?'

'Yes, she's here, come in.'

'Thanks.'

James Bond music drifted in from outside. Data was about to swing on a wire from the rooftop.

'Data, stop!' yelled Mikey, fearfully.

'It's fine, don't worry.'

'Are you alright, Mikey?'

'I'll be fine.'

Within a minute, Data swung from the door frame. 'I'm so sorry.'

'You've broken the door, my door. Mum is going to go crazy!'

'I'm really, really sorry Mikey, just say it was me.'

Just then, Mikey's mother came through the door and demanded that Mikey mend the door. She warned Data to use the back door from now on, then she left again.

Quite by accident, Mouth took everyone to Mr Marshal's attic which was full of valuable, interesting things. He then called Chunk to hold a frame with a map inside it. The map led to a pirate's treasure and the pirate's name was *One-Eyed Willy!*

Mikey suggested that they go looking for the treasure that would pay all their bills. They need not worry anymore. So, off they went on their bikes and rode off at great speed with the map.

It took ages to get to the special place, but the Goonies didn't care. They wanted the treasure so badly . . .
'Where are we, Mikey, in a haunted house?'
'No Chunk, don't be stupid!'
Suddenly everything went black! They felt as if they were being thrown around. They were within a hair's breath of finding the treasure, but now they would be lucky to get out alive. Would they survive? They would have to wait and wait.

For a moment there was complete silence, then a big, huge bang that scared the life out of the Goonies.
'That sounded like a . . . gunshot!'
'No, it wasn't, Chunk, stop imagining things.'
'*Imagining things!*'
'Yes Chunk!'
'Look in the garage now.'
The group looked in the garage like Chunk told them to. Chunk counted to three and the rest of the group were screaming in fright. Chunk then told them to be quiet and to stop being babies but they didn't listen.
'You guys, be quiet please, or they'll catch us.'
The group suddenly froze in shock. Their future looked bleak. They would be lucky to get out alive. Only luck could save them now.

Sophie Brown (11)
Ysgol Y Tymbl, Llanelli

INVISIBLE ANIMALS

It was Tuesday, a bright, sunny afternoon. Jess had an injection because he had a disease which sometimes made him invisible!

He went to work wearing a plastic mask and a long, white coat with a logo on the pocket and a white cap.

In the science room, Jess told Lia that he had an injection and he was now invisible! He took the cap off and the mask and proved to Lia that he was invisible. They tried to make a formula that would make animals invisible too. However, it went wrong. The animals became invisible and they escaped! Jess had to chase them but he could not catch up with them, they were too fast. Lia was very sad to lose all the animals.

Jess made five traps for the animals. he had to catch them all. This was going to be difficult work!

Jess and Lia decided to call for the expert animal hunters. They arrived later that day and went straight to the science room.
They asked, 'Where are the animals?'
'They are everywhere,' replied Jess, who was not now invisible.
'Where? I can't see them,' said one of the hunters.
'That's because they are invisible!' exclaimed Lia.

One of the hunters had an idea . . . 'Let's put some flour on the floor and then we will be able to follow the footprints until we find them.'
'What a brilliant idea!'

Jess and Lia then remembered the glasses and gave the hunters a pair each, so that they could see invisible things. When they put them on they saw a tiger right in front of them. Everyone went off to follow their commands whilst Jess and Lia made their own traps.

After a lot of searching and trekking, they found and caught all the animals. Most of the animals listened to their owners so it was easy enough. The tiger and the cheetah were more of a problem . . .

When they were in sight, Jess dived onto the tiger in order to catch it. He managed to get the net over it (after he'd cut his arm really badly). Blood gushed out from the horrible gash and Jess was rushed to the hospital. In the meantime, the cheetah had escaped again.

Lia knew that it was up to her now. She would have to catch these creatures before someone got hurt. In the distance she saw them racing away. She decided to drive after them with some meat as bait. It was the only thing she could think of.

It worked for a while, but the cheetah went off again. The starving tiger showed an interest in the food. All Lia had to do was tranquillise him and wait for help.

To this day, Lia does not know how the syringes got mixed up, but the tranquilliser worked in two ways! It put the tiger to sleep and made him visible again. Before long the tranquilliser had been used to bring all the animals back to normal. There was just one sad part to this project. Unfortunately the cheetah never returned and Lia felt that she had lost her best animal.

She waited for Jess to recover and they both began a new project. Who knows what it will be next time?

Jonathan Allinson (11)
Ysgol Y Tymbl, Llanelli

DON'T GO OUT AFTER 6 O'CLOCK!

Many, many icy winters and boiling summers ago, fifty to be exact, there lived two bright and sparky 11-year-olds called Elle and Joe. They both had hair like gold treasure and sparkly sky-blue eyes.

On this particular day, they were going to their grandparents' house and were extremely excited as their grandparents were very mysterious and the children had never seen them.

As they pulled up on the gravel-strewn path, they noticed the house. It looked like a tornado had been through it and a bomb dropped at the same time, but that was only one of the spooky things that happened in those 24 hours.

Their grandparents greeted them and told them, 'We are going out now. We will not be back till late. Do not, at all costs, go out and walk after 6 o'clock or you will very much regret it.'
The children didn't listen. The clock struck 6 times and the children grabbed their coats and headed outside. They went down to the marshy ground. The grass they stepped on looked black in the evening sky.

Suddenly a bloodcurdling screech came from somewhere and about 5 slightly shimmering people marched towards them, spookily fast.
One said in a deep, hollow voice, 'You have entered our lair and disturbed our sleep. You must be silenced forever! We must not be found out!'

They had seen enough. The children ran back to the house. As they slammed the door shut they saw an old newspaper article which said: '5 found dead in swamp' and there was a picture of those terrifying people!

Suddenly they turned and watched in horror as the 5 ghostly figures slid into the room and a chilling wind ran up their spine . . .

Iona Hannagan Lewis (11)
Ysgol Y Wern, Llanishen

At The Water's Edge

Alice sat dreaming. She was a simple child, but she had one dream: to be free. To feel the grains of sand trickling through her toes, that was her yearning. Her and her lover, Rhys Capelgwilym had been planning their escape and she expected to hear from him soon.

At that minute, her maid, Mary, came in and announced, 'A note from Rhys.' She passed it across.

It said: 'Meet me on the beach at 6. Rhys'.

Alice smiled to herself and began packing a bag for the exciting event.

The old grandfather clock struck quarter to six. Alice hurried across the hall to the door and opened it. She gasped. The wind was howling like an enraged wild animal and the rain was coming down in bucketfuls. Alice threw herself into the storm.

She reached the beach a soaking wreck. Rhys was there and looked at Alice in a subdued way for a bit. He then spoke.

'Are you sure you want to do this?'

'Positive,' she replied.

They stepped into the boat. Within a few minutes the storm had worsened. Alice was staring, frightened, into the sea when a huge wave crashed over the boat. She screamed and then she blacked out.

She woke up on the beach and Rhys was lying still beside her. By the time she had got help, Rhys was dead.

After the funeral, a lonely-looking figure stood on the beach. The figure stooped and placed a rose upon the upturned boat.

Gwenfair Hawkins (11)
Ysgol Y Wern, Llanishen

A GHOST STORY

Alwena, Alma and Anthea. Triplets. Witty, vivacious daughters of the King and Queen of Welwood. They had everything in the world going for them. If only they had known the fate of the previous occupants, for this had cost one daughter her life.

Alwena woke with a start. She was dripping in sweat. The nightmare had been so real . . . she had dreamed that Alma had been murdered and she was suddenly the only person in the castle. She shuddered at the memory of the awful dream.

She rushed downstairs, eager to see Alma, to make sure she was safe. The only person at the table was a man wearing a bright red balaclava. Suddenly Alwena felt a blow to her head.

Alwena woke again to find herself in a tiny, dark room full of boxes and dusty cobwebs. She pushed her golden hair out of her eyes. She had never been in this room before. Where on earth was she?

She had to get out of this room! She could be anywhere. There was a rusty wooden door at a corner of the room. She struggled out of it.

Alwena ran like a cheetah into the castle gardens. It seemed that everyone had mysteriously vanished.

'Don't scream. There's nobody to listen,' hissed something.

Alwena spun around, her large, dark eyes fearful. A creature made of smoke, with gaping black holes, stared down at her. She blinked and looked at it but the . . . creature had gone. She ran headlong into Anthea. The girls hugged each other, identical eyes staring in terror.

'I've been so worried! Did you see that repulsive smoky thing?' Anthea asked.
Alwena nodded.

The two girls walked hand in hand to the moat and something made them put their feet in. The two pairs of feet touched something cold and slimy. The butler Gilthorn's face came into view.

'Alwena, everyone's in the moat! We've got to help them out!' screamed Anthea.

The girls pulled, heaved and shoved for the next hour, desperately trying to save as many people as possible.

'Look, I've found Alma!' yelled Anthea.

No matter how hard they tried to revive her, she remained stiff. The King, Queen, Alwena and Anthea were sobbing by this time. It was so unfair!

Two months later:
It had been two months since Alma had perished in the moat. Alwena was reading a book about the castle when she found a reference to an old newspaper. It was all about the last royal family, who had been murdered by a sinister, smoky figure rumoured to be a princess who had been maltreated and abused.

Alwena called to Anthea. Anthea smiled sadly.
'So now we know who killed Alma. That girl was so unhappy, she couldn't bear us to have a good time.'

Two smoky figures appeared. One started to turn into a human and very soon 'it' became Alma.

'Thank you so much! I can live again now that you have worked out who killed me. It wasn't really her fault,' Alma whispered, her olive skin glowing with happiness.

The other smoky figure wailed and shrieked loudly as she was expelled into a thousand wisps of smoke that soared into the sky.

'Rest in peace, princess,' said Alma softly.

The triplets went inside to see the King and Queen. All of them smiled radiantly.

Myfanwy Price (11)
Ysgol Y Wern, Llanishen